Michael Veto
THE DARK ENTITY, Book I

All rights reserved
Copyright © 2024 by **Michael Veto**

Published by Spines
ISBN: 979-8-89383-610-3

THE DARK ENTITY

BOOK I

MICHAEL VETO

CONTENTS

It was a dark and stormy night. There were three friends. They were only a couple of years apart and they were also Satan worshippers, and they got a bright idea to fool around with the Ouija board. The friends went to school together.

There was Vanessa Smith. She was twenty-seven years old. She was banging. Her hair was so yellow it was the color of gold and when the sun hit her hair sparkled. She had the perfect body. She had a banging ass; it was nice and juicy and plump every time she walked on the street. She shaked her ass like there is no tomorrow and she stops traffic. She was wearing a C-cup size bra. She had the most beautiful features. She was so hot she put most girls to shame.

Vanessa had a good upbringing. She was brought up to believe that Jesus Christ is Lord and Savior. You must be saved to go to Heaven. So, the church was a Baptist church. She grew up in a church. But all that changed when she turned seventeen. Her parents noticed a dramatic change in her behavior. The biggest one was she did not want to go to church anymore and she stopped completely reading her Bible. They could sense darkness in her. An evil.

Then she met her boyfriend Trey Roman. He was twenty-five years old now but back when Vanessa first met Trey, she was seventeen and Trey was fifteen going on sixteen.

He also was brought up in a Baptist church and it was the same church that Vanessa went to and that is how they met. Trey walked up to Vanessa, and it was love at first sight.

When Vanessa saw Trey for the first time, she saw a fifteen-year-old boy. She loved his face. It was as smooth as a baby's skin. He had perfect eyebrows. Not too thick and not too thin. When they were thinking they looked fake, when they were too thick you look like Grizzly Adams.

He had a faded, skin-tight fade. He was wearing baggy jeans and sagging them. The jeans were black. He was wearing a black and white sleeveless shirt that was twice the size of him, so it would cover his boxers. He sat next to her. He smiled, and she smiled back.

Trey said, "Damn girl, you're fine as hell."

Vanessa could not believe that he had just said the "Damn" word in a church. She was disgusted by what he had just said.

"Wow, you have no respect for the church?" Vanessa asked.

Trey thought about what Vanessa was asking about what Vanessa was asking.

"I respect churches, but I do not believe in the Bible. The book is a bunch of lies. It does not speak the truth. Father Satan is Master and soon the entire world will bow down to Father and the heavens will fall."

Vanessa did not know how to respond to that, so she just shrugged her shoulders her way of saying it was okay for what he said. His looks put her in a small trance. He was hot. She did not want to miss the opportunity to make out with this boy.

Trey said, "So, what's your name?"

"Vanessa. What is yours?" Vanessa said cutely.

Trey said, "I'm Trey and you are so hot."

What Vanessa did not know is that when he put his tongue in her mouth, and he touched her tongue with his, she would belong to him forever.

They were sitting in the first pew on the left in front of the altar. The church was very wide open. The altar was in the center but up against the wall in the back. To the right are eight pews and the windows on the right were painted with glass of Jesus.

The left was the same except there was an exit. There was no one in the church and Trey was starting to feel some type of way and he wanted to leave. His parents were waiting in their black Plymouth mini-van, and they were hoping the girl would come in the van so they could kidnap her.

Trey said, "Vanessa you should let my folks drive you home. We are the only ones here. Let us get you home."

Trey got up and faced Vanessa and took his right hand

out and she instantly put her left hand on to his right and they held hands and started walking towards the exit sign.

Vanessa said, "I have a good feeling about you."

Trey smiled. It was a sinister smile. "Me too."

They walked out of the church and went to a black minivan. The parents were dressed very casually. The father wore just a pair of blue jeans and a white sleeveless shirt. The father was in his late forties. He had thinning black hair, his face wrinkled. He was six feet and one inch tall. He weighed about two hundred pounds.

The mother wore a black skirt, and she had long black hair. The only thing that was white on her was her face and skin where women put lipstick instead of red, she wore black.

As the love birds were coming closer to the minivan, Vanessa wanted to ask Trey a couple of questions.

"Hey, can I ask you something?" Vanessa asked.

They stopped and they both faced each other, and Vanessa grabbed Trey's other hand. Now, he was ready.

"What is up? Ask me anything, Vanessa."

"I can see your build and I approve, and your looks are so hot, your lips are nice and plump. How tall are you?" Vanessa asked.

Trey smiled. "I am six feet tall; I weigh about one hundred and fifty pounds. How much do you weigh and what is your height?"

Vanessa smiled back. "I'm five feet four inches tall and I weigh about one hundred and twenty pounds."

They both kissed on the lips and walked towards the van.

The passenger said, "Jack, it looks like they are coming."

Trey's parents were Satan worshippers. They were Jack and Mary Roman and they were both watching as they were getting closer to the van and now Trey was going to make out with the girl, and they will take off.

Jack said, "I know Mary unlocks that door for them."

Mary unlocked the door. Trey opened the door. He let Vanessa in first and he went in after her then he shut the door.

"Hello Trey," Mary and Jack said.

"Hi, mom and dad. This is Vanessa. She will be mine. I will start kissing her and when I am done, I will cover her mouth with my hand and that is when you step on it." Trey whispered so Vanessa would not hear him.

Jack and Mary looked at Vanessa and they approved of Trey's girl.

The van started to move off the church property and Trey moved next to Vanessa. He took his right hand and put it on her chin and moved it to his face and then he took the same hand and put it behind her right ear, and he put his lips onto hers and she opened her mouth, and he opened him and he put his thick, plump tongue in her mouth, and she touched her tongue with his.

Suddenly Vanessa stopped and she noticed her hair was turning black and her clothes were turning dark black.

"What the fuck is going on?" Vanessa cried.

Trey took his right hand and moved it from the back of her right ear. He put it to her mouth, and he leaned his whole body over her to put the fear of God in her.

"Listen bitch, you belong to me now. Once your hair and clothes are all black you will be my woman and you will do exactly what the fuck I tell you. And in case you have not realized it, this is a kidnapping." Trey said in a sinister voice.

Vanessa could hear evil in his voice. She could hear the deep, sinister in his voice. She felt like the devil was talking and demanding shit from her. Vanessa could not move. She was defenseless. Trey was too strong for her. Her hair was already black, her fingernails and her dress were turning black as well.

"DAD STEP ON IT!" Trey yelled.

The van started moving quickly. Trey looked at his new woman and she was complete. Except she was trying to escape. So, Trey grabbed her by the shoulder and held her tight. His eyes were starting to turn a black color and they were spinning extremely fast.

Trey said, "Look into my eyes."

Vanessa did not have a choice, so she investigated him. She saw his eyes spinning and spinning and it was going faster and faster. Vanessa was now in a trance.

Trey said, "You are under my power, and you are my slave forever. You will do whatever I tell you to do. You will be my lover and have my babies. You are no longer a Christian. You will worship the Father Satan. You will denounce God. You will bow to me and call me Master. Your name is Vanessa Smith. It is Katie Kole. Do you understand?"

Vanessa was now weak. "Yes, Master I understand."

So that's how Vanessa and Trey met. The third person is a person that they met, and his name is Matthew

Connor. His past does not matter, he was a scumbag. How Trey and Vanessa (also known as Katie Kole that is if she was in a trance) met Matthew was when he answered an ad online. He had just bought an Ouija board and he wanted to invite people to play with the board with him.

His Ouija board was all black even the letters on it were black and the planchette was all black with a clear circle in the middle to see if there were spirits around them. Most people who messed with the Ouija board thought that it was a game and that is the mistake that most people make. When they think it was a game the most common mistake was thinking that demons were not real, or they were trying to connect with loved ones that have passed to the other side.

These three had one agenda and only one agenda. It was on a more sinister side and that is to open the gateway to Hell and conjure demonic spirits and to let them fester their lives and for demons to walk on Earth. When they did this these two demons came through the gateway. That was Vale and Vetis.

Vetis would have one of his friends and make him kill his friends and make him kill his friends and that is exactly what he did. It was Matthew Vetis had. Matthew lured his newfound friends into the bedroom that was next to the kitchen.

He had a sharp knife with a handle that was all black and had the pentagram in the middle of the handle and it was all red, blood red. He went up to Vanessa, took the blade, and slit her throat. The blood was gushing down like a waterfall, she was gasping for air and her defenseless body fell to the ground when she hit the ground there was a big thud.

Then he walked over to Trey, and he did the same thing that he did to Vanessa, and he took the same blade and slit his throat and again the blood was gushing down like a waterfall and the blood was hitting the rug on the floor of the room. He was gasping for air, and he fell to the ground and when he fell, he hit the ground and there was a big thud. Both Trey and Vanessa were in a pool of blood. Matthew laughed and had a shit-eating grin on his face.

Then Matthew took the bloody knife that he murdered Trey and Vanessa with. He took the blade to his throat and he started to walk, wobble towards the back wall of the room so evil could keep the gateway open. He slit his throat, and he sprayed blood all over the wall and fell to the ground. All three bodies and souls got sucked into the middle of the Ouija Board. It was as if nothing had happened on the Ouija board that was on the kitchen table. The planchette went down to the word Goodbye. Until someone decides to open that portal and that was going to be sooner than the world would know.

TWO

Two brothers were walking around. They were walking towards the Lynn Woods, where they were told not to go too late at night. The parents told them that there are strange things that happen in those woods. But they were kids, they were curious but, on this night, they were going to unleash an evil that was going to take thirty-five years to get rid of. He was always watching over his younger brother, sometimes he encouraged him to do risky business.

The two brothers were ten and twelve. They loved Halloween. They loved everything about it, the ghouls, the goblins, and the horror movies on television. Jason Starr was twelve years old. He was always watching over his younger brother, sometimes he encouraged him to do risky business.

Jack Starr was ten years old. He looked up to his older brother and they always got into mischief. When they got into mischief, they loved terrorizing people in the city and now it was simply egging houses, robbing houses, stealing bikes, and stealing lunch money from kids in school. When it came to that these kids were a bad combination together and no one fucked with them. If people did not give up what they wanted, they simply beat them up and took their stuff.

The boys wore big, baggy jeans. It did not matter what color. They also wore long, big shirts to cover their boxers. The reason is because they always wore their jeans below the waist. This was called sagging. Their mother did not like the way they wore their clothes. She hated it; but the father believed if it made them feel comfortable then they should do what they felt, to be different.

They terrorized the city they went to from egging houses on Halloween, to bullying kids at school. They both attended the same school, and they would fight the other kids just because they could. There were a couple of times they got caught and that happened because the kids they beat up ratted on them. In other words, they told the teachers about them. They got suspended but the father did not do anything because of the way he looked at it he did not raise wimps, he raised tough guys their mother knew better not to interject.

The city and the school knew it. Then they decided not to fight anyone unless it was called for. They decided to rob the weakest kid and they took his lunch money. If the kids refused to give up when they demanded their stuff, they beat the shit out of them and took their shit. When they did this the kids, they robbed never told them again and that was because they threatened them.

Then they got sick of the fact that they did not see the

thrill of it anymore. So, they got into robbing houses. Now Lynn was a big city and they started to scope out houses and when no one was home they would break in and rob them. They stole everything small enough to fit in their duffel bags. They looked for money lying around, jewelry. They always took expensive rings and necklaces. The necklaces had to be 14K and up.

They also looked for game systems, VCRs, and DVD players, which were just coming out and only rich people had them. They also looked for laptops. They always wore gloves, so their prints would not be all over the place. It only took them five minutes to rob a house and by the time the owners got back they would not know they had been robbed until a week or two later. Then after that, they found that to be too boring. So, they increased the risk, and they started stealing bikes and they did that for some time. They found that was too easy. Everyone was leaving their bikes unattended and unlocked.

So, they got into purse snatching. They were so quick that the purse they were stealing the women could not find them because they worked as a team. Jack would talk to the victim and Jason would snatch the purse. Jack would go in the opposite direction, and they would meet up. After a while, they would find that too easy.

So, they were getting bored, so they would walk around, and the city knew they were always up to no good. They had never been caught for any of their crimes. When the boys walked on the bricks.

The bricks were another way of saying streets. When people walk on the same side of the street they know what their actions are, and they are up to no good. They also know their parents will not do shit; they are afraid of them.

So, they will quickly cross the street, and if they are women, which in most cases, they are, they will hold on to their pocketbooks for dear life. These people are afraid of their brothers.

Jack and Jason tonight were wearing all black and big, baggy clothes. They were walking up to Lynn Woods. Jack was always there to back up his older brother and that is because he wants to be like Jason, and he enjoys terrorizing people. Now they were getting close to Lynn Woods and saw this other boy and Jason knew him. He knows him because he is in some of his classes at school.

One day Jason was in the study hall, and he overheard him talking to another classmate that his family is rich, and they always give him three hundred dollars a week for an allowance and the classmate was wondering why he was telling him that. Jason also overheard the classmate tell this rich kid that he should not be bragging about how much he gets in a week. The last thing he said was that his classmate told him that's how people get robbed. The rich kid told the classmate that would never happen. Jason had a big shit-eating grin on his face.

"That's what he thinks." Jason laughed.

The classmate was good friends with Jason and Jack and the classmate told him what the kid had said. He told him that his name was Jonathon Connors. The classmate told Jason he was bragging that his family is rich, and he gets a three hundred dollar allowance a week, and he was jealous. Jason assured him that he would take care of it. He was going to wait for the perfect moment, and he was going to roll up on him. Jason heard the entire conversation. How Jason takes care of it, he was going to rob him.

Jonathon was walking down past Lynn Woods as Jason and Jack were walking up. Jonathon took his money out of his front right pocket and started counting it. Jason saw it. He stopped in his tracks and looked.

"Jason, what's up bro?" Jack asked.

Jason said, "Look at this kid and tell me what he is doing?"

So, Jack looked up and saw this boy counting his money out in the open.

Jack said, "You mean that nerd with the pocket protector in his right breast pocket of that white, long, sleeveless shirt that has the top button buttoned, which is tucked into his tight jeans that look like high water? With a butch haircut. "He looks like a bitch and a fag!"

Jason grinned. "Yeah, I know him. He is in my homeroom at school and bro, he was bragging to one of our friends in school that his family is rich, and he gets three hundred dollars for an allowance every week and our friend was jealous. He told me about it, and I told him I would take care of it."

Jack said, "Damn bro, there must be at least six hundred dollars in his hand."

Jason said, "Listen, bro, what we are about to do is going to start a trend in this city, and in years to come people like us, thugs, will follow us in what we are going to do."

Jack was having a tough time following him. "Bro, what did you have in mind?"

"What we are going to do is bully him and put the fear

of God in him. We are going to tell him to run his shit. If he tries to get away, he will not be able to move because we are going to block him. I am going to walk up to him, and you will walk behind him so that way if he tries to get away, we will ambush him, and take his money. I will do all the talking and you will back me up to make him give up his money." Jason said confidently.

Jack said, "No problem. He is a bitch. He is going to bitch out and if he knows what is good for him, he will run it. So, we are robbing him? Is that what running your shit means bro?"

Jason nodded his head yes. "Let us do this."

So, Jason and Jack walked quickly up to Jonathon, so they could rob him. Jason walked in front of Jonathon and Jack walked behind Jonathon. Now Jonathon had a bad feeling about what was going to happen next.

"What is this?" Jonathon asked nervously.

"Hey Jonathon, what's up? Do you remember me?" Jason asked.

"I remember you." We were in the same school and the same homeroom together. What do you want?" Jonathon asked.

"Okay, I will get right down to it. You got me up close and personal and my brother was right behind him. He is so close to you right now you can hear him breathing in you. So, if you try anything or try to escape, we are going to beat the shit out of you!" Jason said fearfully.

Jonathon was getting scared. His stomach felt like a knot in his stomach. People feel this way when they get nervous about certain things. He was so scared he started to shiver and shake. His body was starting to tremble. He had sweat coming down both sides of his face. The sweat was dripping down his head where his hairline and face met. He started to cross his legs. He could feel at any moment he was going to piss his pants out of nervousness.

Jonathon could hear Jack breathing behind him, and Jason was an inch from his face and there were no cars and no police. It was a perfect spot nice and dark, and no one was around as witnesses.

Jonathon was getting the feeling that something bad was about to happen. He could feel nervousness all over his body and his bones. He now knew that these guys saw him counting and flashing money. He knew he was about to be robbed.

"What is this man?" Jonathon said.

"Run your shit bitch! In case you are too dumb to figure out what is happening we are robbing you. You like to brag to kids we know in school that your family's rich and they give you a three hundred dollar allowance every week. How much have you got?" Jason demanded.

Jonathon felt goosebumps all over his body. Now because Jason was an inch from him, and Jack was an inch from him in the back. Jack was so close to his back that he felt the heat on the back of his neck. Jack was breathing so hard that Jack swore he would melt in the frigid weather. But it is October, it is still fall and winter does not happen until December 20th.

Jonathon said, "How much do I get?" For two weeks I have six hundred dollars on me now. What? You are robbing me?"

"ARE YOU FUCKING DEAF? RUN, YOUR SHIT BITCH!" Jason demanded a second time.

Jonathon said, "But I need this money. My mom gave it to me."

Jason was getting pissed off and he wanted the money. "I DON'T GIVE A FUCK WHO GAVE IT TO YOU, NOW YOU ARE GIVING IT TO ME RUN YOUR SHIT BITCH! GIVE IT UP! I'LL FUCK YOU UP AND TAKE IT BRO!"

"BRO' LISTEN TO MY BROTHER IF YOU DON'T GIVE IT UP YOU WILL GET FUCKED UP BEYOND RECOGNI-TION AND AFTER WE FUCK YOU UP, WE GONNA TAKE YOUR MONEY. SO, YOUR BEST BET IS TO RUN YOUR POCKETS! "JUST GIVE IT UP SO WE DON'T HAVE TO FUCK YOU UP!" Jack chimed in.

So, Jonathon was outnumbered, and he had no other choice but to run into his pockets. So, he went into his front right pocket took his money out, and handed it over to Jason with no problem. Jason had the money in his hands, and he smiled at Jonathon. Suddenly Jonathon was so scared and nervous that he started to piss his pants and the pee started to trickle down his right leg. He honestly thought these guys were going to fight him and or jump him and fuck him up.

"Thanks for letting our classmates know that you get a three hundred dollar allowance every week. Because now our people are going to rob you every week because you are a bitch and I just proved it. Hey bro, let's bounce. Hold on!"

Jason noticed his pants. There was a wet spot. He started to giggle because he knew what this bitch had done. He was so scared that he fucked pissed his pants out of fear. He was walking like a fucking sloth.

Jonathon left and continued to where he was going, and Jack and Jason let him pass and they continued to Lynn Woods.

"Here's your share bro. You did an excellent job making him run through his pockets. You got that bag that has the Ouija board in it?" Jason asked.

Jack said, "Of course I do. You see it in my pack, right?"

Jason said, "Stop being a smart ass. Here we are: the Lynn Woods."

Jack and Jason knew the issues with Lynn Woods, and they were not afraid to enter. They thought the stories they heard about the woods were a crock of shit. So, they entered the woods. When they entered the woods, they noticed a tall, rusted gate. At the top of the gate, it said: Lynn Woods, and below that it said: *Lynn, Massachusetts*. The gates themselves had skulls on each side of the gate as a doorknob. This would be the last time anyone would see or hear from them again.

As they were walking, they could not see anything. It was like a black hole in the park. It was so dark that they could not see anything in front of them. They heard a lot of noises from different animals and so on. They saw a good spot to play with the Ouija board. Well, at least they thought it was a game. That's the biggest mistake people make about the Ouija board. They sat down, and Jack unzipped his black backpack and pulled the Ouija board out.

He set it on the ground as both brothers were sitting

next to each other. Their Ouija board was something Jack made by hand. It was not the typical Ouija board but just as dangerous if you are not careful.

Jack took out the planchette he had set on the board. He placed it on the G spot of the board which is the middle of the Ouija board. Both boys put their hands on the planchette, and Jack appointed his brother Jason to ask the questions because he was the older brother he started with.

"Are there any spirits out here that want to communicate?" Jason asked.

The only thing is they thought they were going to conjure good spirits. But they were about to unleash a demon that had been locked on the Ouija board for over one hundred years. What they did not know was that when they opened the portal to the Ouija board it would be exceedingly difficult to defeat. It is like when you let the genie out of the bottle but try to put him back in the bottle it will be exceedingly difficult to do the same as the Ouija board think of the Ouija board as one big portal and one big bottle.

The boys waited for a minute. Then without hesitation, the planchette started to move on its own. At first, Jason thought Jack was moving the planchette and Jack thought Jason was moving it. They both stared at each other.

It moved to the letter H and then to the letter I to spell the word Hi.

Jason said, "Hi, are you a boy or a girl?"

The planchette moved to the letter B then to the letter O and finally to the letter Y which was spelled Boy.

Jack and Jason were excited to communicate with the dead. They did not see any harm in it, so they continued.

Jason said, "Are you good?"

There was a long pause, but the planchette quickly moved. The boys still had their hands on the planchette as it was moving to the top left of the board which said: No. The boys felt that their hands were super glued to the planchette.

Jason said, "Are you evil?"

The planchette moved to the top right which said: Yes.

That did not scare the boys and they continued playing where most people would say good-bye, but they did not. They were intrigued and once again they did not see any harm in it.

Jason said, "What do you want?"

Where Jason and Jack were, there was enough lighting for them to see the board and what it was saying.

The planchette moved to the letters J-A-S-O-N and then it went to another set of letters J-A-C-K. When they saw the planchette spell out their names they could not make heads or tails of what was going on. They honestly thought this was a game. They started to realize that this was for real. They had a challenging time keeping up with it. Now the boys were freaking out and Jack did not want to play anymore.

"Jason, I do not want to play anymore. It is getting real. I am scared and I have a bad feeling something unbelievably bad is about to happen." Jack cried.

Jack was trying to warn his older brother about what was going on. He had a feeling for what was going on there and he feared what was happening. But Jason was not trying to hear it. Jason was the tough guy between the two of them. Jack was feeling some type of thing about this.

"Stop being a pussy! It is only a game!" Jason said sternly.

"No, it is not just a game! This is for real this is about our lives! I heard a story that Mom and Dad told me right before I went to bed and the story goes that in the seventies there was a kid my age to be exact and he went into Lynn Woods these woods and he fucked with the Ouija board and when they found him, he was like frozen solid out of fear and his hand was glued to the board. So, do not tell me it is just a game!" Jack yelled.

Jason said, "Listen, bro, that is only a story. It is not real. They only told you that, so you would not wonder in Lynn Woods by yourself that is all just a story."

Jason looked down at the Ouija board and he was getting furious. He wanted to know where this thing was. So, he asked the board another question.

"Where are you?" Jason asked confidently.

The planchette moved to another set of letters B-E-H-I-N-D Y-O-U.

The boys started to look around. They broke the circle and let go of the planchette which is a big no-no.

Jack said, "Oh my god! What the fuck?"

Jack saw the demon. He was all black, he was like charcoal, he looked like he was burning on a bonfire. He was completely bald and his eyes were bright red and they got bigger and brighter as he crawled towards them like a three-year-old. But his arms were muscular and as he was moving his arms Jack could hear the bones cracking. Then what got him was when the demon started to stand up all his bones started to crack, and it was loud it sounded like a branch from a tree breaking off. Then Jack saw the demon getting taller, it was as if he was growing.

He saw horns that just grew on each side of his head. He had sharp, very sharp teeth. His canines were starting to grow. They were as sharp as Dracula's teeth but sharper. He was starting to grow a tail that was as red as fire and at the end of it, there was an upside-down arrow, and it was pointing down towards Hell. His body was all red and black mixed, his muscles were like a bodybuilder. His arms were three times that of an average human. His muscles were huge. They were as big or even bigger than people on steroids and people who lift weights. He started to grow red and black wings. He had a black halo on his head. His eyes were as red as fire.

Jason said, "What is it?"

Jack said, "He is right behind you." I told you we should have stopped. I told you we should have stopped. The bastard is right behind you bro."

Jason turned around and he could feel the evil that was unleashed on the Ouija board. The entity sucked the life out of Jason. As he was sucking the life out of him, Jason was in midair choking and there was nothing Jack could do to save his brother.

The entity was done with Jason, and he started to transform himself into something else Jack could not make out. But when he looked closer, he was not transformed. He was getting taller and bigger. Jason's lifeless body fell to the ground within seconds. Since the entity was out of the Ouija board, he was free.

"Who are you?" Jack asked.

"I do not have a name I am a powerful demon, and I am the thief of souls of the living and the dead. I am going to take your soul and kill you. Give it to me!" The demon demanded.

The demon lifted Jack with the point of his right hand and brought him over to him. Jack's mouth opened wide, and the demon opened his mouth and sucked the soul out of Jack. Jack could not move. He was gasping for air, but he knew it was no use. Then the demon dropped Jack and he landed on top of his brother. The demon sat up the boys against a tree and put both of their hands on the planchette of the Ouija board so whoever found them would know they died from using the board.

As the demon was leaving, he was looking back and suddenly, the boys and the Ouija board vanished out of sight and out of mind. They vanished without a trace. Rumor has it that this was the same demon that killed that ten-year-old boy back in the seventies.

The demon was transforming back into a little child riding a two-headed dragon. He was sitting on the back of the dragon in between the red wings of the dragon. The demon jerked back and started to whistle. The demon and the dragon were flying and fading into the midnight hours of the night. They disappeared into the darkness of the black hole.

The boys were never seen again. They searched but they could not find them. The police looked for three weeks. It was as if they had disappeared from the face of the earth.

If you walk through Lynn Woods sometimes you can

hear the creepy voices of Jack and Jason Starr. The family was not happy with the investigation. They felt that the police could have done more but there was not much more they could do. You can hear the boys every Halloween night yelling to help them, and the demon has a grip on them, and he is strong he will not let their souls go. They are imprisoned. The demon that killed Jack and Jason was Valoc.

Some of the residents of Lynn were glad they were gone because now they can rest easy and not worry about being egged, beaten up, purses snatched, or robbed.

The city closed Lynn Woods and reopened it thirty-five years later. The evil never came back...Well for the rest of the season, it did not return. It came back a year later. But not in Lynn. It was in a more haunted city where witches were hung.

CHAPTER

THREE

Jacob Master was brought up as a Catholic but in his teenage years he was not into going to church. He wanted to start his own thing. So, he decided he was going to worship Satan and he loved serving him as a boy. He did illegal things, smoked pot, and drank with his friends. One night his parents had enough of his shit. So, they thought at first that it was a phase, and he would grow out of it when he turned eighteen, they saw he was still acting strangely, and they saw he was not going to change so they thought they would have a little talk with him, to see where he is. But that got worse when they told him he had a week to get out of their house.

Today is Jacob's eighteenth birthday. He went into his room and his room was on the same floor as his parents'. His room was all black. He painted all four walls the darkest black he could find, his curtains were black as well, his bed sheets and blankets were black as well, even the carpet in his room.

He had an altar in the center of his room that had books on Satan worshipping and a black cloth that covered the white cobblestone altar. On all four corners are four black candles. In the middle of the altar is a pair of black gloves. To the left of the gloves is a satanic dagger which is super sharp. It was so sharp that it could cut through the skin. To the right of the gloves is a white plastic cup that holds blood.

Jacob knelt before the altar and said a couple of prayers to Satan to give guidance in what he was about to do. He was going to kill both of his parents. He was going to start with his father, and he was going to put his blood in the big cup. If his mother interferes, he will knock her out. Then he will cut his mother's throat and take her blood.

He got up and put his gloves on took his dagger and put it in his left back pocket. He grabbed the tall white plastic cup, and as he was leaving his room there was a white eight-ounce bucket. He grabbed it and went into his parents' room, and he saw they were both sleeping. He took his dagger out put the cup on the edge of the bed, and held it in position with his right knee. Then he put the dagger on to his father's throat and slit his throat with one hard slit and the blood was dripping down in front of him, he thought it was going to drip on his side of the bed.

So, he moved the cup to the front of his throat and the cup was getting filled with blood as Jacob's father was gasping for air. The blood filled to the top of the cup and Jacob pulled the cup away and put it in the big bucket. Then he went over to his mother, and she also was sound asleep, and he slit her throat with the dagger, and he put the cup in front of her to catch the blood. Her eyes opened in shock.

"Jacob." She gasped. As she was trying to gasp for air.

"Yes, mother!" Jacob said in an eerie scary voice.

Then she could not say anything else. She wanted to, but she could not. She tried to say something.

"Sorry Mother what did you say? I cannot fucking hear you!" Jacob replied in a sinister voice.

Jacob was getting more sinister. The reason for this is that a demon has a hold on him, and he is not letting him go. When Jacob denounced God that's when Satan came into his life and took over him.

But he knew her life was over, and blood filled his cup to the top and he walked around to his father's side where the bucket was, and he dumped her blood in it. He had what he needed for a Satanic ritual. He walked back into his room, and he had a gold chalice on the altar. He then walked to the bathroom which was in the middle of the hallway that connected to the bedrooms and the kitchen.

He walked into the bathroom went to the cobblestone sink and washed out the white plastic cup. He washed it well. So, there was no smell or blood stains in the cup, so he soaked the cup with hot water and bleach and set the cup in the far-right corner of the sink. The bleach he got out of beneath the sink. But before he did that, he took off his black gloves and there was a box of rubber gloves. They were yellow, they were specifically for cleaning the bathroom and he put them on.

He poured bleach around the sink and scrubbed it. He did that so there would be no traces of blood on the sink.

He wanted it to be the perfect murder. Then he dumped the cup in the porcelain toilet and then he flushed the toilet twice and then he rinsed the cup out twice and smiled. He took off his gloves and put his ones on. He took the yellow gloves and disposed of them. He walked out of the bathroom and took a left and a sharp right to his room and he shut the door. He had his black Satanic robe hanging on the back of the door and he put it on. He was ready to bless the blood in the name of Satan.

"Oh shit! I left the cup in the bathroom. I need to get it!" He spoke.

So, Jacob opened his bedroom door and took a right into the hallway and then he took a left into the bathroom, and he saw his cup on the sink, and he grabbed it, and he could smell the bleach in the bathroom.

He chuckled. "The smell of bleach what a great smell. Nothing is going to stop me now." He spoke.

He walked out of the bathroom with his cup in his right hand and took a left his robe was flying quickly around the corner, and he took a sharp right to his room. He walked in and shut the door. He walked to the alter and he took the black lighter that was in his right front pocket, and he continued to light all four black candles. The reason he has black candles instead of white candles is that black candles stand for evil and darkness, in most cases white stands for godly, good, and pure. Jacob picked up the eight-ounce bucket that had blood from his parents in it and he recalls it being very heavy. He had to use two hands on the handle to lift it. He put it on the left side of the altar and he was careful not to spill it on the black carpet. It was midnight black. Finally, he was able to set it on the altar.

He grabbed the Satanic chalice, and he dipped the chalice in the blood and that was his sacrifice; his goal; was to be as close to Satan as he could. What made Jacob so dangerous was that he was very fluent in Latin and that is what Satan spoke. Jacob could even speak it backward.

He could only imagine what God and Jesus were thinking of him at this moment in time. Jacob is not afraid of dying nor is he afraid of Hell. He cannot wait to see Hell, so he can serve Satan and be with him eternally. When he was younger, he already said the prayer to have Satan on his side and for him to come into his life.

On a piece of blank paper that was on his bed. He walked over to the bed and grabbed the notebook, and he took a piece of paper out of it, and he grabbed a pen that was to the right of the notebook.

Then on his bureau were three pieces of incense that smelled like sapphire, so he lit them and started to wave them throughout the room. He did this to open the gates of Hell. So, he put one on the wall next to his door, and another one went on the wall on the left side of the room. While they were burning, he was writing to Father Satan.

Jacob finished the letter and he saw this: his candle holder was all silver with his black candle in it along with the four black candles already on the altar. He also noticed the chalice with blood on it was also silver, so he was about ready to say the blessing and the ritual. He was dressed all in black and his robe was in black too. The incense burned ten minutes later.

"Okay it's time for demons and Father Satan to come into our world and come into me and make me do evil things," Jacob said.

Jacob needed one more thing before he could begin, it was a silver bell that was in his parents' room, he opened his bedroom door and walked out of his room, and he took a right into his parent's room, he saw the silver bell on the bureau when you first walk in the bureau is on the right. So, he grabbed it and went back into his room, he shut off his bedroom lights and walked over to the altar so he could begin. He needed to invoke the crown prince of hell. He rang the bell and faced east. "Father to the east."

Then he rang the bell again and faced the north. "Beelzebub to the north."

Then he rang the bell and faced the west. "Astaroth to the west."

Then he rang the bell and faced the south. "Azazel to the south."

Jacob knelt before the altar to show Father Satan respect. Then he recited the invocation prayer.

"In Nomine Dei Nosteri Satanas, Lucifer excelsi.

In the name of Satan, Ruler of the earth, True God, and Almighty and ineffable, which hast created man to reflect in thine own image and likeness, I invite the forces of darkness to bestow their infernal power upon me. Hell, the gates of Hell come forth to greet me as your brother and friend.

Deliver me, O mighty Satan from all past error and delusion, fill me with truth, wisdom, and understanding, and keep me strong in my faith and service, that I may abide always in thee with praise. Honor and glory be given thee forever and ever." Jacob said.

Jacob grabbed the chalice very carefully and brought it to his lips and he drank the blood and put it back on the altar. He grabbed his paper and the letter he wrote to Father Satan, and he fell to his knees as if someone pushed him to his knees he looked at his paper and read the letter and he put a lot of heart into it. When he finished reading it, he could feel dark energy in the room. He saw blue energy filling the room and heard a voice calling him.

When Jacob turned around, he did not see anything, but he heard the voice again. It was a voice in his head. Then the voice was very eerie. It had a deep dark voice and at first, it scared him. It was an actual whisper.

"Jacob burns the paper and I'll take care of you." The voice said.

Jacob put the tip of the paper and the flame caught the paper on fire he put it on a white dish that he had on the alter and he set the burning paper on the dish, and he watched the paper burn and he noticed that as the paper was burning the flame was turning from a red to a light color and at the moment, he knew that one of the colors was blue. Then the paper stopped burning and he was looking around, and he wanted to know where Satan was.

"Father Satan, where are you? I know you are here. Can you please show yourself?" Jacob said.

"I'm right behind you." The voice said.

Jacob turned around and he saw a tall man. He was wearing a black suit. He had a black dress shirt on with a bright tie and he was wearing a black fedora.

"I am Lucifer, but you will call me Father Satan. You belong to me." Father Satan said.

Jacob was surprised, and he looked closely, and he could not believe what he was seeing. He did not picture Father Satan as a man wearing a dark black suit, a black dress shirt with a bright red tie, and wearing a black fedora.

"Your father is Satan? I do not understand. I pictured you a little differently. I pictured you as a demon. A creature of some sort. I pictured you all red, with horns on your head, a trail on your behind, red wings, and a blue halo above your head. With razor-sharp teeth. I did not picture you like this." Jacob expressed.

"Do you approve? The reason I look like this is because in your mind this is how I look. Innocent looking but evil at the same time. I am here to take you to your resting place. We must go because if the police officers come over here due to nosey neighbors and they will see what you have done they will put you away for good." Father Satan said.

Jacob was not surprised. "I approve. I only killed my parents because they were interfering with what I was doing. They were going to separate us from what we were doing and they would not let me be. So, they had it coming."

Father Satan said, "I know I must take your soul, so I can bring you to Hell, and that way you can be one of my demons." Bow to me. Go on your knees."

Jacob went on both his knees. "Yes, Master."

Father Satan said, "You are no longer Jacob Masters." You are a demon. The demon of death. You will also be called the Angel of Death. Once you get close enough to the living you can also put them in a trance and make them do what you want them to do and take their souls. Once you own them you will be able to kill them."

Jacob understood Father Satan put his right hand over Jacob and his soul was coming out of his body and it was going to Father Satan and when it was completed, Satan laughed, and he vanished. Jacob's defenseless body fell to the floor.

The soul of Jacob now belongs to Father Satan, and he is now the Angel of Death. He is one of the many princes of Hell and he is an extremely dangerous demon. His job is to team up with Valoc and Vetis and take control of the living. That is exactly what they do.

FOUR

It was Halloween night and Rodney Marks was about to do trick 'n' treating. Most folks would tell you he was a bit old for knocking on strangers' doors to trick 'n' treat. Rodney was eleven going on twelve, but he was short. He did not look much older than seven or eight.

Rodney was dressed as an angel from Heaven, and he took his plastic Halloween bag that had pictures of grey tombstones on the bottom of the bag to make it look like it was a cemetery. On the tombstone it said, RIP engraved in the middle., leaning against the tombstones were those big Jack 'O' Lanterns on the right and the left of the tombstones there was a witch on her stick of the broom and the witch was wearing all black and had an ugly green face with sores on her face she looked like the witch from *The Wizard Of Oz.*

She was flying through the dark sky and passing the

full moon. He dumped the bag on the table beside him. It weighed like a ton of bricks. The bag was filled to the rim.

His mother was in the bathroom. She was getting ready to go to bed. You know what women do? The bathroom was small. It had one small shower and next to the shower was a white toilet bowl. The only thing that was not white was the handle on the left side which was silver. Then when you walked into the bathroom on the left, there was a mirror and a porcelain sink that was under the mirror. The tiles were cobblestone, but they were not the real thing. The bathroom was next to the kitchen. Rodney's room was also, and his parent's room was only across the way.

Joshua Marks was the captain of the Salem Police Department. Tonight, it's going to change everyone's lives dramatically. A couple of weeks ago...Joshua found that his wife was having an affair with one of the police officers on the force and what hurt him the most about this whole thing was that it was his befriend who did this to him.

Joshua was rummaging through Rodney's candy making sure there was no loose candy and making sure all wrappers were on the candy. Once he saw everything was good, he tapped his son on the back of his head.

"You're a good kiddo," Joshua said.

Rodney took his candy and put it back in his bag and he went into his room for the night. He was exhausted and he fell asleep face first on his bed his face was in his pillow.

Maggie was coming out of the bathroom. She had

long, beautiful goldfish-colored hair when the sun beats down on it shimmers and glitters. She had a perfect skin complexion; she had an average-sized head, her eyes were a light green color, and she had a body to die for. It is no wonder why all the police officers were staring at her. Some people could not understand why she would marry a police officer especially a bastard like Joshua. He was always verbally and physically abusive towards her.

As Maggie was coming out of the bathroom Joshua did not say two words to her. He was disgusted with her, he was disgusted with her, he felt betrayed that his wife would do that to him, he was trying his best to avoid her. Maggie was afraid of her husband. This man was huge, he was very muscular, and she knew that he knew of ways he could kill her and make it look like either an accident or they were self-inflicted and that was because he was a police officer. Could he commit murder? Who knew?

She said, "Darling I am tired. I am going to bed early."

Joshua said, "Okay."

Maggie checked on their son and then she went to bed. She lay flat. Then she fell asleep. Joshua sat at the kitchen table he thought about killing his wife and once he did that, he would have no other choice but to kill his son he would be a potential witness if his father got prosecuted in court then he had another dilemma, and that was what would he do next? The thought of killing himself would be better because he has two bodies in the apartment and to escape prosecution offing himself seemed the best choice. He figures after he shoots his wife and son in the head where he knows the bullet would lodge in their brains, he could sit at the kitchen table and put the barrel of the gun in his mouth, and pull the trigger.

Joshua had his black Beretta 9mm and he got up from the kitchen table and walked into his and Maggie's room. She did not hear him come in as she was sound asleep. He walked over to her on the left of the bed and shot her in the head where the brain was. The bullet traveled through her head it did a clean break through her skull and penetrated her brain. She flinched as she was soaked in a pool of blood she died instantly.

Joshua said, "Fucking whore!" He stared at the body out of disgust. As he was disgusted, he shook his head to the right jerked to the left, and put his head down.

Joshua left the bedroom and walked over to Rodney's room. He was expecting him to hear the gunshot but to his surprise, Rodney was still sleeping on his chest.

When Joshua went into his son's room, he started crying. He did not want to kill his son, but he knew he had to because he would have been a potential witness. Joshua blocked his pistol back.

He said, "I am sorry son. God, please forgive me for what I am about to do."

Joshua went up to Rodney and shot him in the back of the head. The bullet went through his head, pierced through his skull, and lodged in his brain. He flinched, and he drowned in a pool of his blood. He was dead instantly like his mother.

Joshua could not believe what he had done. He did not care about what he did to his wife, and he felt she deserved it after she cheated on him with another police officer. But what he did to his son he could not live with himself. He knew there were a few bullets left in the chamber, but all he needed was one to do the job.

Joshua sat down at the kitchen table, and he was crying but he knew what he needed to do. He put his pistol in his mouth and pulled the trigger. The bullet went right through his brain and there was blood and brain matter all over the back walls and under the kitchen sink. The apartment looked like a blood bath. Joshua was dead and there is no coming back to that.

A neighbor called the police after hearing the last gunshot. The police knew the address all too well. When they got there, they opened the door and Joshua shot himself. They saw his wife was shot once in the back of her head. After the police investigated this horrific scene, they concluded that Captain Joshua Marks shot both his wife and son. Then he turned the gun on himself. The motive is unknown. They ruled it murder and suicide. Case closed.

People can only guess what happened here, but it would not be factual only a belief or an opinion on what happened.

What is clear though is that Joshua Marks was a good husband, a loving father, and a good police officer. No one will ever know what drove him to kill. Residents believe he got evil from the city of Salem. But on Halloween night you can still hear Maggie and Rodney crying and asking why he did this to them. You can also hear Joshua crying and saying he is sorry. But not sorry that he killed Maggie.

He will always feel that she is a bitch. Sometimes though if you are outside of the apartment complex and if you look up it has been said that around 11:59 P.M. you can see all three of them walking aimlessly around the apartment. Some people think they are waiting for the next tenant to haunt them.

CHAPTER

FIVE

The town of Hope, Massachusetts was small. It was out in the boondocks. The nearest store will take you twenty-five minutes to walk, but five minutes by car. Without a car, it would be exceedingly difficult to travel. This town again was so small that everyone knew each other. If someone committed a crime in Hope even though the Police Department only has two police officers one of them being the chief of police. But the surrounding towns will help.

That is where Linda Carmichael and her two boys would host parties. She had a light grey A-frame house. When you walk on the three steps on the side of the A-frame which has a door that leads to the kitchen. There were no windows on the kitchen door. In front of the A-frame are two sliding glass doors. When you walk through the doors it leads you to the family room.

To the right is a brown lazy-boy recliner. It was such a light color brown you could mistake it for tan. Next to the lazy boy is a couch that flips out and makes a bed. Across from the couch is a twenty-five-inch plasma smart television. Movie applications are already built into the television. Next to the television on the left is a stove to heat the house during the winter months. On the right is a set of stairs that lead to two bedrooms. The rooms are across from each other.

The room on the left had two beds in it. A small television is in front of the bed on your left when you walk in. Between both beds is a tall, dark brown dresser. Which opens, and the drawers are inside.

The room across the way was for one person. One bed, one bureau, no television. Linda's older son had a room with two beds in it. Her younger son had a room across the way.

If you come back downstairs and walk through the family room and take a right and your first right that's where Linda's room was hers and her husband's. Her room was huge. This woman had everything in her room. She had the largest room in the house. Her bed was in the middle of the room; her closet was to the left of the bed. Her walls were painted a light blue which is her favorite color.

On the right of the bed is an oak end table where she can put her books, anything she can grab in the morning.

Across from the bed was her bureau which was made from real maple oak, and it was big and heavy. On top of the bureau was an eighteen-inch flat-screen television. Underneath the television was a grey cable box.

Her closet was huge, and it was a walk-in closet. She had so much room that it was not even funny. Going to leave her room, you take a right, and going down the hallway you will stumble across the kitchen.

On the far right of the kitchen are two windows, to the left of the windows is a white refrigerator and across from the refrigerator is an electric stove, the ones that have glass on the top and you cannot see the burners unless you turn the stove on. The dials were all black and the timer numbers were all right. The temperature for the oven is in the middle, it is all electric. There were cabinets next to the refrigerator. There were six cabinets on the left and three cabinets on the right.

Towards the door is the kitchen where Linda and her family would share meals. She had pictures of flowers, pretty pictures the women liked. There are four windows in the kitchen. One by the refrigerator and the stove. The other one is on the right side of the kitchen table; the last window is on the same side as the grey-painted door. The floor is a light brown cobblestone color with little specs of black on it.

The bathroom is right next to Linda's room. She loved the yard. It was huge, and she used to have summer, spring, and fall parties outside. She had winter parties inside. She had to sell the house because her husband was killed in a car accident.

Once that happened, she could not afford the mortgage on the house. So, she packed up and moved to Lynn Massachusetts on June 17, 1991. She had rough times, but she got through them. Something happened to her, and it was something she would never forget.

SIX

It was a little party that Linda was having. She had a party at the beginning of spring, the beginning of summer, the beginning of fall, and the beginning of winter.

She had a lot of people over. People were drinking beers, hard liquor, and mixed drinks, and some people brought party favors. When you walk into her apartment you could smell the aroma of marijuana. To most folks, it smelled great, but Linda could not stomach the smell of pot, but she still was a good host. Then you had people snorting cocaine. White is a white powder and some kids if they see it, will mistake it to be snow. Out of respect for her kids, they did not do it in front of her two boys.

Linda was in the kitchen, and she had a few things on the stove and in the oven. She went to check it at the same time as the party. She was getting dinner ready when she cooked. Whether it was dinner or anything else she cooked for an entire army she would have leftovers for days sometimes weeks. Her family never went without her.

Ever get the idea that someone is watching your every move? Well, that's how Linda felt. She could feel eyes on her, and she could hear someone breathing hard on her. The person that was doing this his name was Robert Shaw. He was her ex-boyfriend and he was pissed that she broke up with him. He told her that he was going to get revenge on her, and she laughed at him. She did not believe that he was capable of even doing what he threatened. That also took all the energy going to hurt her, so she took his threat with a grain of salt.

He grabbed a knife. The same knife you would find in the kitchen to cut meat and veggies very sharply. It was on the wall next to the stove. He had the knife in his right hand which was behind his back, and he grabbed her long auburn hair and yanked it back in a jerking move.

"I TOLD YOU BITCH I WOULD COME BACK AND HURT YOU, BUT YOU FUCKING LAUGHED AT ME! YOU DIDN'T TAKE ME SERIOUS! YOU MADE ME LOOK LIKE A FOOL IN FRONT OF EVERYONE AT ONE OF YOUR PATHETIC PARTIES! NOW YOU ARE GOING TO MEET YOUR MAKER!" Robert yelled.

No one heard him yelling and he took his right hand from behind his back and jabbed the knife through her chest. He was aiming for her heart. He was hoping that the knife would penetrate her chest cavity and go through her heart. Blood was gushing down the front part of her body. She was bent over just a tad, and she screamed in agony. The knife hurt her so badly she did not want to pull it out because if she did, she would make it worse. She was fighting for her life.

"You motherfucker! You are going to pay for this you son of a bitch! You're a fucked in the head who stabs someone for breaking up with them! If I live through this, you are dead!" She yelled.

It took all the energy that was in Linda to say that and then she fell on the kitchen floor. All you heard was a loud thud. She was on her back, and she turned her head to the right in a downward position. She looked lifeless.

Robert heard footsteps coming down the long corridor that connected the living room and the kitchen. As the footsteps were coming closer and closer, Robert ran out the back door which was in the kitchen then he slammed the door.

A tall man was walking through the corridor. His name was Chris Samuels. He was well over six feet tall, and he wore baggy clothes even though his pants were loose fit and baggy edition he always sagged them. He loved to sag his pants and no one in the city fucked with him and that was because thugs in the city knew he was tall and that it would be hard to rob him, so they never tried.

But Chris loved to rob people. He always targeted the weak, the ones that wore their pants to their waist, and the ones that wore tight jeans. To him, they looked like a bitch. He knew people like that. He did not need a weapon to rob them. All he had was to step up to them and say one phrase and that is what he would say, "RUN YOUR SHIT!"

When he did so they wouldn't even attempt to fight

him so they would empty their pockets, and give up all their money, their cell phones, if they had watches, and expensive jewelry. He also took their wallet and he would take their wallet and he would take their ID and told them he was keeping the ID so if they tried to call the cops he would know where they lived and he would visit them this is the reason why Chris was the most dangerous thug in Lynn.

He was approaching the kitchen and he saw Linda on the kitchen floor. She was bleeding like a sieve, and he ran to her, and he could not believe what he was seeing. It was a horrific scene.

Robert was already outside, and he was in the backyard. She had a small yard, which is why she would have parties inside her apartment because her yard was not big enough to fit everyone back there. There was a fence in the back.

The fence was grey, and the tip of the fence was very sharp. When Robert ran away after he stabbed Linda, he got a nasty cut from the fence on the palm of his right hand. Beyond the fence is a little stream of water. He took the bloody knife he used to stab Linda and threw it into the stream. Then he ran away from the complex. The reason he threw the knife was because he knew the minute the knife hit the water, his fingerprints would not be on it. He also knew that if there was blood on it, the water would wash it away and the knife would sink. He was hoping that if the police were called, they would not find the knife.

When Chris entered the kitchen and saw Linda on the kitchen floor bleeding, he ran over and fell to his knees to see what had happened. He was hoping she had enough strength left in her to tell him what had happened.

"Linda, what happened?" Chris asked.

She was having a tough time getting her words out. Every time she tried to speak, he could see blood coming out of her mouth. He knew he had to call for help.

Then she whispered in his ear: "It was Robert Shaw, my ex. He did this to me. I did not even see this coming. He grabbed my hair and jerked my head back..." She said as she was gasping for air.

Chris continued to see blood coming out of her mouth, and he also saw the stab wound. Blood was gushing out there very quickly and he knew he had to do something. She was losing a lot of blood. He needed to act quickly. It was no longer a thought it was necessary. He got up and walked over to the door in the kitchen that leads outside and grabbed the white cordless phone that was mounted on the wall. He dialed 9-1-1 on a single ring and someone answered right away.

Emergency dispatch said, "911 emergency. This is Officer Jenkins. This call is being recorded and monitored. What's your emergency?"

Chris said, "I'm calling because my friend has been stabbed in the chest. She is losing a lot of blood, she's bleeding from her chest and there's a lot of blood coming from her mouth and she's gasping for air."

As Chris was telling emergency responders what was happening, and he was losing his breath himself he could feel his anxiety racing through his body and in his chest, and at the same time he could not believe this was happening. Suddenly, he had a lot of rage and anger. The emergency operator could sense it.

Officer Jenkins said, "Sir, right now I want you to take a few deep breaths and I know this is hard, but I want you to try to relax and you got to be strong for her. Okay?"

Officer Elizabeth Jenkins was a 27-year-old police officer. She worked as a dispatcher for the police department. She had the sweetest voice, and she was exceptionally good at her job. She knew how to talk people down when they call hysterically, she had an act for it, and she loved to help people in need.

So Chris took a couple of deep breaths. Officer Jenkins could hear him taking a couple of deep breaths. She was glad to hear about the deep breaths he was taking. The deep breaths she could sense he was taking.

Officer Jenkins said. "Can I please have your name?"

"My name is Chris Samuels," Chris said calmly.

Officer Jenkins said, "Okay Chris. Now that you are calm and collected, the anxiety is gone. Can you give me the address of the emergency, so I can send the emergency responders?"

Chris said, "The address is 73 Woodman Street, Lynn Mass."

Officer Jenkins said, "Chris, hold on a second. I am typing it as you are telling me. What's the victim's name?"

Chris said, "Her name is Linda Carmichael. Please hurry, I am looking at her right now. She is turning pale. She does not have much time."

Officer Jenkins said, "Chris, I already sent the emergency response team over. They should be there soon. What I want you to do is continue to stay calm you are doing good and stay on the line with me until they get there."

Chris said, "Okay."

Chris could hear the sirens of two cruisers and an ambulance, and they stopped in front of the apartment complex.

Chris said, "Ma'am the police and the paramedics are here. Can I hang up now?"

Officer Jenkins said, "Yes, you can Chris. Hang in there."

Both parties hung up.

There was a knock on the door. It was more like someone made a fist and banged on the door loudly. The party was silent, nobody moved, and they stayed where they were. They had no idea what was going on. They had no clue what had just happened to Linda.

"Who is it?" A woman's voice asked. She said it very nervously. She did not know what to expect.

"It's the Lynn Police Department! Open up!" The police officer demanded.

The woman who asked was at the door and got up from the brown loveseat that was in the middle of the living room against the wall and the rest of the guests gave her a look like they did not answer the door. They were thinking that because they had party favors, and they thought the police were there for that. She paid no mind, and she answered the door.

When she opened the door, she saw a tall man wearing a light tan suit with a pair of black shiny shoes. He was young-looking, and she started to twirl her long black hair. His mahogany brown hair was parted to the left side; he showed her his badge.

"Ma'am we got a 9-1-1 call from this address that someone had been stabbed and we need to get to her where the kitchen is." The police officer said.

By the time everyone was quiet they were all shocked at what the police officer told them. It was so quiet you could hear a pin drop. Everyone in the living room knew right off the bat that Robert Shaw had done this.

The reason they knew it was him was because of the last party Linda had. She broke up with him and in the living room, he told everyone at the party including her that he was going to do whatever it took to hurt her even if it meant killing her. No one took him seriously. Linda and everyone else laughed at him. The people who were over at her house when the stabbing happened were the same people when Robert threatened her and the same people who laughed at him.

The woman who opened the door for the police pointed to the corridor and he peeked through and saw the kitchen and the victim lying on the kitchen floor. He walked in and behind him was a uniformed police officer and he stood in the living room. He was in the middle of the room holding his gun on the right side of his waist as if someone was going to pull a fast one.

The Lynn police wore all black with a blue stripe going down the left side of their pants. The badge was silver which was on the top left of the uniform and the badge, said: *Lynn, Massachusetts*, and in the middle of the badge was their badge number. At the bottom of the badge is the word *Police*.

On the right side is the officer's last name and they were doing something new: Below their name, they were putting how many years they have served in the police department. On the right shoulder, there was a patch that said Lynn Police Department. At the bottom of the patch, it said Lynn, Massachusetts. The left side was reserved for their rank.

The uniform police officer did not have a rank, nor did it say how long he had been in the department. He was fresh out of the academy, a newcomer, and this was his first day and case.

The third person that came in was a paramedic. He went right to the kitchen; he had his big red first aid kit. The bag was strapped to his right shoulder. He was wearing a white buttoned-up dress shirt with black slacks on; he had black shoes on were slip-resistant shoes that were needed. He had a patch on the right side of his shirt that said EMT which stood for Emergency Medical Technician.

He was big, not fat but very muscular. He walked into the kitchen, and he saw Linda on the floor. He could see her chest still moving up and down. He was amazed that she was still breathing. The paramedic ran over to Linda and started to make an IV for her. He was wearing blue latex gloves.

"Excuse me, sir...?" He asked the police officer.

"Oh, I'm sorry my name is Detective Simon Veratrole," Simon said.

"Detective, I need space to work; this woman needs immediate medical attention. The gentleman that is by her can stay." The paramedic said.

Chris started to cry. He thought he was going to lose his friend right before his eyes. The paramedic administered the IV into Linda's left hand he grabbed some clear tape and put it over the IV needle. He looked at Chris and he put his hand over his right shoulder letting him know that his friend was well cared for.

The paramedic gave Linda a pain killer, so she would not be in pain. He could not take the knife out because if he took it out it could damage the main artery in her heart.

He went back to the ambulance, got a stretcher, and took her to the hospital which was down the street. It was on Boston Street and the name of the hospital was Lynn Memorial. It used to be called Lynn Hospital. The hospital administration was thinking about changing the name and that was because they were thinking about moving the hospital to Union Street but that wouldn't take place for a few more years.

"Hey sir, can you stay with her while I go to the ambulance and get on the stretcher? I will get my partner. He is just finishing a few things in the ambulance. Keep talking to her. What mostly works is telling her a story about an enjoyable time you and she had." The paramedic advised.

The paramedic got up and left the kitchen and walked out to the ambulance. He walked out to the ambulance he walked quickly. It was a matter of life and death, so he had to move quickly.

Chris leaned forward and started whispering in Linda's left ear. He was hoping that she could hear him and remember what he said.

"Hey, honey I do not know what to say. I have never

done this before, but the paramedic told me to talk to you and that is what I am doing. Hey, do you remember the time when I was younger, and you caught me egging the neighbor's house and the people came out and saw me doing it? The husband came out in his boxer briefs and yelled at me, and you did not like the way he spoke to me. You were feeling some type of way about the situation. So, I remember you told me you went to his door, and you said kids will be kids it was a typical Halloween prank and I also remember the stupid bastard tried taking you to court for the way you spoke to him. But nothing came out of it."

Chris grabbed her left hand and said, "Squeeze my hand if you can hear me."

She did not squeeze Chris' hand. He started to get worried when he saw that her chest was not moving up and down to show that she was breathing. He started to freak out he was starting to sweat a lot and when this happens it was never a good sign it always meant he was getting anxious he thought this bitch was not going to die in front of him.

The paramedic came back and went into the kitchen and had the stretcher with him and this time he asked his partner with him, so he could help him put Linda on the stretcher.

"My name is Alex, and this is my partner, Jonathon. "Alex said.

Alex was the paramedic that started the IV on Linda and Jonathon was a little on the heavy side and sometimes it took him a little to get to the scene, especially if it was on the third floor.

One time Alex and Jonathon went to this one place and the elevator was not working so they had to climb four flights of stairs to get to the patient. It was at the Lynn Housing Authority which was on North Ocean Terrance. By the time he got to the apartment, Jonathon was breathing hard and at times lost his breath. He had to stop to catch his breath. Alex thought he was going to have a heart attack. The company they worked for ordered Jonathon to get a physical just to make sure he was physically fit for the job. He went through a lot of tests, and it said that he needed to lose at least a hundred pounds before he could return to work; he also had to quit smoking. He quit smoking and he joined a gym five months later and he lost weight. He still belongs to the same gym today and he is still smoke-free.

Chris said, "Alex she is not breathing. Do something, please. She cannot die because she has kids. Two boys would be crushed if she died. They are remarkably close to their mother and they have no contact with their father."

Alex said, "Listen we will try to revive her. What we need to do is get her on a stretcher and to the hospital. We have a machine that will restart her heart in the ambulance."

Chris knew they were going to try to save her and revive her. So Jonathon and Alex lifted Linda onto a stretcher. She was heavy. Her body was lifeless. When that happened it was because she was dead, but they were not going to let her die. They strapped her to a stretcher and wheeled her down the corridor into the living room. They had an oxygen mask on her and an IV was putting fluids in her.

When the paramedics brought her through the living room everyone wanted to know what had happened to Linda. The police informed everyone to stay calm and that they had everything under control. They also said an investigation was going to be conducted. The paramedics carried Linda down three flights of stairs and wheeled her into the back of the ambulance. The ambulance took off to bring Linda to the hospital with sirens blaring for everyone to get out of the way.

Chris was distraught and he had a feeling something like this was going to happen, but he never thought it was ever going to happen like this. Chris was there when Linda humiliated Robert, and he was the laughingstock of the party. She made him feel like an ass. This usually happens when Linda gets hammered, she does not realize what she is saying and the next day when she attacks someone, she does not remember it which is why she should not be drinking. She cannot manage alcohol. She only gets like that when she drinks hard liquor. Chris and the detective sat at the kitchen table. He took his small notepad out and put it on the table.

Simon said, "Okay sir let's talk about what happened here today. I don't want to make you feel uncomfortable so tell me, what did you see?"

Chris said, "Okay, Linda was in the kitchen getting dinner ready. When she cooks anything she usually cooks for an entire army. I was in the living room chilling with my boys and shit and we were sucking down some cold ones and shit. I did not see anything out of the ordinary until Robert Shaw came over. He was Linda's ex-boyfriend, and he swore revenge on her. I mean no one thought he was serious so there was no action necessary to take. Detective, I am going to be fair and honest with you. I am a thug and I hate the police. I am talking to you because I want you to catch this prick and if me and my boys get a hold of him it will be all over."

Detective Simon was writing everything that Chris said on his notepad when he took out his right-side pocket. He said, "Tell me more about Robert Shaw. Tell me why they broke up and the last time he was here was before today. I want to know what led up to this."

"Wait you think she deserves this? I know what you are going to do. You want information, and you are going to find a way to use it against her, aren't you? This is the reason I cannot stand police officers when it comes to stabbing. You always think the girlfriend always deserves it when their ex either beats the shit out of them or stabs them." Chris said sternly.

Chris was now really pissed off. He felt the police officer was going against Linda and he was not getting a good vibe from him. But he still wanted to hear what the police had to say.

Simon said, "I am deeply sorry you feel that way but listen Chris I am on your side and I want what you want. But I need your help, so we can catch the guy. Trust me, when we dust this kitchen with prints, we will find two sets of prints. One will be Linda Carmichael's and the other set will be Robert Shaw's. So, please help me and I will promise you that no one will know that you are helping us in this case. So first tell me what this man looks like."

Chris said, "Okay first I have a question for you. How do you know my name?"

Simon said, "I know your dad. He was a good man. I miss him. He is the reason I became a police officer, to begin with. He was a good influence on me when I went to the police academy. That is how I know who you are. Let us get down to business Chris. So, describe him to me."

Chris said, "Okay here goes nothing. Robert Shaw is like five feet, six inches tall. He has thinning brown hair, pot marks on his face, and acne problems. When he was younger people used to call him Crater Face or Mr. Pizza… and they still do. He always wore tight blue jeans with a white tee shirt tucked in. He does that so his package will bulge, and it is also to show off his ass. He wears these big, thick, black-rimmed glasses they are the ones that look like from the fucking eighties."

Simon was jotting down the information, and he needed the uniformed officer to call it in, so they could catch this guy.

Simon said, "Let me call for the officer to come in here, so he can call in the description of this guy. Officer! Officer, can you come to the kitchen please?"

The officer heard that he was being paged to the kitchen. "Sorry folks I must go to the kitchen. The detective is calling me. You may go about your business."

When the officer turned around and started walking towards the corridor towards the kitchen everyone who came over to Linda's party split.

The officer's name was Jack Summers. He was a newcomer, and he was young. He was the youngest officer on the force, and he was gung-ho about getting the bad guy. He was the type of police officer who would do exactly what it took to get a collar which means a bust. Jack walked down the corridor and entered the kitchen.

"You called me, Detective?" Jack said.

Simon said, "Yes, I need you to radio in the description of the perp I want this guy in custody. But when you radio it in, make sure they put on the bulletin that he could be armed. He is extremely dangerous dangerous. Make sure they take caution when approaching Robert Shaw."

Jack said, "Yes sir."

Simon gave the description to Jack and with the radio that was clipped on his left shoulder, he radioed it in. He did it so Chris would be at ease and to show him they were doing their jobs.

Jack leaned his head to the left towards the radio and pressed the black button on the side of the radio with his left hand.

Officer Summers said, "Car 15 to base."

Dispatch said, "Base 15, go ahead."

The dispatcher was a woman's voice. She was African American, was in her late twenties and she just had a baby. She had to work on her anniversary. Her name was Jackie Coles. She was about five feet, four inches tall, and weighed about one hundred and twenty-five pounds.

Jack said, "Base I am at 73 Woodman Street, and Linda Carmichael was rushed to Lynn Hospital in critical condition. Ms. Carmichael was stabbed through the chest and slightly pierced her heart. I have a description of the suspect in question and a name."

Jackie said, "Okay give me the information you have Officer Summers."

Jack said, "His name is Robert Shaw. He is five feet, six inches tall, he has brown thinning hair, he has pot marks on his face which would leave scar tissue damage, and he is wearing a pair of big, black-rimmed glasses from the seventies. He may be armed but he is extremely dangerous and use caution when officers approach him."

Jackie said, "How old is he?" What is his date of birth?"

Jack looked at Chris. "Sir, by any chance do you know his date of birth and his age?"

When Jack asked Chris this his hand was off the button on the radio.

Chris said, "He was born on March 12, 1955, which makes him forty years old. He just turned forty. I know this because he is older than Linda."

Jack pressed the black button on the side of his radio.

Jack said, "Base Mr. Shaw is forty years old. His date of birth is March 12, 1955."

Jackie said, "I just punched him into our database and this man is going to be tough to find for two reasons. One is he does not have any priors and the second reason is whoever this man is he is not who he claims to be. Robert Shaw died five years ago; his death is unknown. They just closed his case last month."

Jack said, "Hold on! Are you telling me this man is deceased? What is going on here? Something does not add up."

Jackie said, "That is correct he is a deceased officer from Summers. I do not know what is going on but what I do know is that something does not add up. I am sorry."

Jack said, "Thank you. Okay, ten-four."

Jackie said, "No problem. Over and out."

Simon said, "Okay Officer Summers I am going to fingerprint the kitchen and find out what is going on here. You can wait in the living room for me. I am almost done with her."

Simon got up and started to fingerprint the back door in his left hand was the brush and in his right hand was black powder. He opened the square stamp-like container that had black powder to take fingerprints. He dipped the brush and applied the brush in two strokes, and he saw one set of prints. He grabbed some tape to capture finger-prints. He put the tape over it and sealed it, bagged it up, and tagged it.

Simon put his hands in the air because there was nothing else he could do for them. He was getting aggra-vated. He wanted to do more for them.

"I got the print, and I am going to send this to our tech lab to see who stabbed Linda. But there is not much more we can do. You heard it on the radio. We do not even know who the guy is but please tell me more about our mystery guy. But we have a print, and this will tell us who the perp is if it is not Robert Shaw." Simon said.

Chris was fucking pissed. He could not believe what he was hearing. He knows the police are trying to do their best to find whoever oversees whoever did this to Linda Carmichael. So, he would do what he had never done. He was going to tell Detective a story about the mystery man.

A story that no one knew about, but Chris did, and the police will also find that the reason Linda broke up with this guy was because of him.

Chris said, "Detective let me tell you a story and it is going to give you a huge picture about this guy, and after hearing what I have to say you might know who I am. I am not buying that bullshit over the radio. Take your pad of paper out and take notes on what I am about to tell you. You will see what type of monster he is."

Simon took out his pad of paper and took his pen out of his right ear and he opened the pad of paper.

Chris was ready to tell the story of what he knew to be true only because he had seen it firsthand.

"Okay, there are a few things you should know about this guy who claims to be Robert Shaw. I first met Robert when Linda first brought him here and her kids got a weird vibe from the guy. Just to let you know kids can sense evil before adults can and the same with animals. Linda has cats and every time he came into the main area of the apartment, he would always act funny. Like there was something off about the guy but at first, I could not figure out what it was. I mean there were several times that Linda told me that there was something strange about the motherfucker. So, one day I had to know so I sat down with Linda, and we stayed up all night talking about what was wrong with this guy.

"She was telling me that he always had a challenging time getting it up, so she suspected the guy was homosexual but that's not what bothered her about the guy. She didn't like the idea that he would correct her children and her on various occasions that they felt like he was watching them, and they were afraid he was going to do something horrible to them.

"Her older son who is Chris Carmichael said to her one night that he was going to do something horrible to them and he had a vision one night while he was sleeping that he was going to stab her.

"But she ignored it. She told him to stop talking about that nonsense and she assured him that was not going to happen, and it was because there were too many adults and if he tried something he would not get extremely far. There were a few other things wrong too that did not match up. He lied about where he came from. Naturally, Linda believed him because he was around her age and at first this man did everything for her.

"He lied about insignificant things like where he went to school, where he worked in the past, and of course, the big one lying about his sexuality. He always avoided questions like that he did not even cuddle with her in bed. Every time she kissed him on the lips when she was not looking, he would wipe the kiss off his lips.

"I saw a lot of shit he did, and she did not approve of him smoking pot and snorting cocaine in front of her kids. So, when the kids told her what he was doing while she was not there, she did not believe them and that is because every time she had a new man in her life, they would destroy her relationship with a new man. When they came to me about what they told Linda I was so upset with her, so I confronted her. I asked her why she would not believe her kids about what this guy was doing. She told me that kids tend to make up stories just to get under their skin.

"So, finally I told her she needed to get rid of him. I told her he was no good for her and she knew sexually there was something wrong with him, but she did not want to let go. She had this crazy idea that she could fix him meaning she could turn him straight. I told her that she had a better chance of seeing God before that happened. She thought about it and realized I was right.

"She called him in the bedroom. The only people that were in the bedroom at the time were Linda, Robert, and me. She was afraid of him when she was talking to him and when she was about to tell him it was over, she was shaking like a leaf, but she did not show it or at least she tried not to. I was in there in case he tried something.

"She told him it was over. She asked him not to come over here anymore for the sake of her kids. At this point, she could not trust him. He packed his bags and moved out. We never heard from him again until today."

Simon said, "Well, that is some story but that does not ring any bells in my head." What I am going to do right now is write an incident report and after I am done writing it, I will have you look at it. You can read it over and if everything is right what you have said. I will have you sign it after you do that. I will give you a copy to hold on to for Linda and when she gets out of the hospital you can give her a copy. I will file my copy with the department. While I am doing that, I will send the fingerprint to the lab and when I get news about it, I will personally tell you."

Chris was pleased to hear that something was being done in one way or another and he did not feel that it was a waste of time for them to be there. He was happy that they were taking this seriously. Most other police officers would not give a shit. They would take only about ten minutes and they would find ways to get underneath your skin. Some police officers do not like hearing the truth.

So, here is what happened at the end of this case: Linda got out of the hospital two days later but while she was in the hospital Chris and her two kids felt a presence in the apartment. It was an evil presence and what they thought happened was when Linda got stabbed, she died on the kitchen floor.

The first night the two boys were home without their mother. They were scared, but the babysitter was more afraid than the boys. It was Chris Samuels who was watching the boys. He remembered it as if it had happened yesterday: The boys were sleeping, Chris and Shayne. It was late, it was ten minutes past one in the morning. Chris heard Shayne talking to someone, so he got up from the loveseat in the living room to check it out. It sounded like it was coming from the kitchen when he heard Shayne referring to the person as his mother.

When Chris walked down the hallway he got slapped in the face with a foul odor. It smelled like flesh was being burned or falling off someone's body. As he got closer and closer to the kitchen the smell got stronger and stronger and when he finally got to the kitchen, he saw a person that resembled Linda. But he knew it was not her, it could not be her. She was in the hospital.

Chris said, "Shayne who are you talking to?"

Shayne acted surprised by Chris's question. He looked at Chris as if he was an idiot.

Shayne said, "Chris, you cannot see her? It is Mommy. Can't you see she's out of the hospital?"

Chris said, "Shayne, that thing is not your mother. That thing is a demon who took the form of your mother. Your mother is fine, she is in the hospital resting. Tomorrow we will call the hospital, so you know she is okay. Now go back to bed."

Shayne went back to bed. Chris saw the entity and he was confused about how this could happen. He was scared, and he knew who could help. But the problem was that she lived in Salem, Massachusetts. It would take her a while before she could get a babysitter, she was Linda's best friend. These two did everything together and the other reason he did not want to call her was because it was late, so he decided not to call her.

An hour later, Chris fell asleep on the loveseat. He was having what he thought was a dream about what happened when Linda got stabbed. He saw the stabbing as if he was right there when Robert did it. The strange thing was it was not Robert doing it. It was a demon.

The demon was the president of Hell. He was the thief of souls and he also enslaved the souls of the living and the dead. When he saw the stabbing, he noticed that Robert Shaw had helped. Chris in his vision saw something else that was behind him, forcing him to commit this crime. People would think Chris and Linda were weird if they were told what happened.

The whole apartment was dark and evil. Chris was walking around; he saw Linda lying on the kitchen floor bleeding. Her soul came out of her body, and he saw himself trying to help her and bring her back to life. He also saw the paramedics administer first aid to her and put her on a stretcher. Then he saw himself talking to a police detective about what was going on.

Chris said, "What the fuck?"

A voice said, "Hello Chris."

Chris heard the voice, so he turned around and saw a woman who looked like Linda, but he knew it was not her. She was in a white dress; it was a wedding gown. Her face was mangled. She was the ugly woman Chris had ever laid eyes on.

Chris said, "Who are you, you demon? Unclean spirit!"

The spirit was getting angry, her eyes turned red. Like she was possessed, or she was purely evil.

The spirit said, "I am Linda's spirit. It is going to rain on earth forever and there is not anyone in this world that can stop me. I will tell you one thing Sage will not work on me and this will be the last time you see me. If you think you are thinking if you move, I will not follow you. That is your first mistake. I already knew you were thinking of calling Linda and telling her."

Chris said, "You have no idea who you are dealing with."

He took off his crucifix from around his neck. He put it towards her. The crucifix was made of 14k gold, and he made the sign of the cross towards her in the air.

He said, "In the name of the Father, the Son, and the Holy Spirit in the name of Jesus I condemn you back to Hell. You are a fucking bitch!"

The spirits started to scream.

"I'LL BE BACK!" it yelled. Then she vanished in thin

air and Chris went back into his body and he woke up. At first, he thought it was a dream. He knew he had to tell Linda what had happened, but he knew he had to tell her before the unclean spirits returned.

Linda was in the hospital for a while. She had died five times and finally, she was stable. She spent three days in ICU which is an Intensive Care Unit. After three days she spent another week in the actual hospital. She returned home, she saw her kids and Chris Samuels, but Chris never told her about what he had experienced.

He would wait four years before he got the courage to tell Linda what happened to him, and what Shayne experienced while she was in the hospital. The problem would be that she would not take his word for it.

CHAPTER

SEVEN

Once again it was party time. Linda was putting one on to welcome the spring season, she was preparing dinner, and her kitchen was genuinely like her apartment at 73 Woodman Street. She was nervous about being in the apartment. Everything about the apartment was the same as the last one.

The format of the kitchen was the same as the stove and the color of it. Where the back door was and even where the kitchen table was right next to the tree. That is because ironically the same person owns both apartment complexes. The only difference was that it had a pantry. In the pantry was a sink to wash dishes, which was an odd place to have a sink.

There were three bedrooms. One was hers which was adjacent to the kitchen, the other room was near the pantry that belonged to her younger son Shayne Carmichael. The third room was in the middle of the corridor. That one belonged to her older son Chris Carmichael.

If you leave the kitchen, you go to the living room and through the hallway. The room was on the right. Her living room was the same size as her other apartment.

Her love seat was against the white as snow recently painted walls. It was in the middle of the wall. In front of the love seat was a square stained coffee table and across from the table was a white-painted table; it had a thirteen-inch size television on top of the white table. Underneath the television was a small black cable box from a local company.

Chris Samuels walked into the kitchen, and he saw Linda was cooking and he thought he would keep her company. He also thought this would be a suitable time to bring up what he saw at 73 Woodman Street. When she was in the hospital.

He also thought it had been four years since she was able to manage what he was going to tell her. Nothing prepared him for the reaction he would get from Linda.

He also noticed she was nervous to have people around as she was still mentally recovering from when she got stabbed and the fact that the police could not find the bastard that did it.

Chris said, "Linda how are you doing today?"

Linda said, "Well I'm doing okay but I wish they caught the bastard that stabbed me four years ago."

Chris saw how Linda was acting. He was thinking about how he would be able to manage what he saw. He was thinking about what he witnessed when she was in the hospital. When he heard Shayne talking to the parasite, he was debating whether to tell her what happened while she was in the hospital.

Chris was also toggling in his mind how he was going to tell her and at the same time, he was thinking about how she was going to manage it. He did not want to scare her either because she had been through. But she had the right to know.

Chris said, "Linda I have to talk to you about something. Some events happened while you were in the hospital and I must tell you."

Linda said, "Chris I don't want to talk about what happened four years ago. It's bad enough that the motherfucker stabbed me and the fact he got away with it and the police were no help."

Chris said, "Listen, the police tried to get this guy. He fooled everyone. No one knew who he was, but I know the whole story and I can explain to you what happened. I saw the events that happened after you got stabbed. I saw you getting stabbed. It was a vision I had. I need to tell you about it before it is too late."

Chris was hoping Linda would listen to him and take the time to act after he tells her the story, but he knows she will think he is full of shit. At that token, he does not want to scare her because if he scares her, he will hate to see how she would react. If she gets scared, he is afraid she will move and if she moves, he cannot go with her because he has everything in Lynn. His job is here, his doctors are in the city, his therapists, and most importantly his boys are here. In Salem, it is harder to run people's pockets, and in Lynn, it is easier because people in Lynn are always flashing it and they are likely to give it up.

Linda said, "Okay but first I must check on Michelle. I will bring the radio out here so if she cries, I can hear her."

Chris sat at the kitchen table and waited for Linda. She went into her bedroom. Hers was the biggest room in the apartment. Her bed was in the middle of it, next to her closet. It was ridiculously small, and she could not fit all her stuff in the closet.

To the left of the room which was near the closet was her white bureau and it was tacky. It was not painted right there was only one coat of paint on it. She had two windows to the far right of the room. She did not have a nightstand because she did not have a lamp. Her light was on the ceiling fan. The lights were above the ceiling and the fan was underneath the lights. She loves it better than an air conditioner. The ceiling fan keeps the room cooler faster than an air conditioner and it saves her money on her electric bill. To the right of the door were two circular switches. One was for the lights and the one next to it was for the fan.

Michelle's crib was to the right of her bed and was in front of the windows. Her crib was nothing special it was all white, and she had toys that hung above her, she saw her mother and she smiled at her, and she started to laugh to indicate that Michelle was happy to see her mother smile back and made some silly faces to make her baby laugh again. Linda bent down and kissed Michelle on her forehead.

Linda wound her toy that was dangling above the crib and when you wound it up it played a children's jingle, and the toys would move in a circular motion, and she would be able to hear the jingle and that would relax and put Michelle to sleep.

Then she grabbed the radio which was all white and the volume control which was blue on the top. Then she left the room and right before she left, she saw her daughter and saw she was sleeping again.

She slowly closed the door. She did not want to wake up Michelle. She came to the kitchen table but before she did that, she shut her tan stove off but kept the oven on because she had a pork loin in the oven. She had on because she had to cut the loin in half and put it in two different pans and Linda always does that her party does not start until eight o'clock tonight.

So, she walked over to the kitchen table sat down, and was ready to hear what Chris had to say.

Linda said, "Okay Chris tell me a story."

Chris said, "Okay Linda the story I am about to tell you may terrify you and I want to apologize ahead of time, but I must tell you about it because it deals with us and the reason you moved here from 73 Woodman Street. It happened after you were stabbed.

"The first night you were stabbed you were in the hospital I heard some commotion in the kitchen it was late. I was watching television in the living room when I heard the noise, and I turned the television down I heard Shayne talking to someone and I saw the unclean spirit to which he was talking. The unclean spirit was you. It was evil you. But the way I knew it was a demonic entity was when I got off the loveseat, I was walking down the hallway and as I was walking down the corridor there was an odor that had a nasty stench. It smelled like the flesh was dripping and melting off the bones of the body like when you see in horror movies where the flesh would catch on fire, and it would melt away.

"As I was getting near the kitchen the stronger the smell would get. It was so bad I started to gag and when I finally reached the kitchen, I saw Shayne talking to the evil spirit. I asked Shayne who he was talking to, and he told me he was talking to you, and he gave me that look as if I was surprised to see the spirit and I knew you were not dead because if you were I would have known about it.

"I would have gotten a call from the hospital indicating that you passed away, so I knew that part was not true. I looked at the being now and I did not see the demon face to face. All I saw was a dark shadow figure that in a way resembled you. This thing smelled bad. I told Shayne to go back to bed and I told him that this thing was not his mother and I promised him that we would call you.

"An hour later I fell asleep in the living room on the love seat and the strangest thing happened: I had a vision. The vision was me walking down the hallway, but it was weird. Everything was dark and there was no light, there was no sign of good, it felt dark and evil. Now this is where it gets weird.

"When I walked in, I saw Robert grab you and stab you. He was being controlled in some way or form. I looked closely and he was coming out of the bedroom and there was something else behind him. It was a demon. He was the president of Hell, he was the thief of souls, and he enslaved them to do what he wanted them to do. So, what

I am thinking is that Robert Shaw is dead, but his spirit is very well alive. I do believe his soul was enslaved to a dangerous and powerful demon.

"In the vision, I saw myself and the detective and the paramedics working on you and the pool of blood that was over the kitchen floor, you flatlined. So, I took off my necklace that had the crucifix of Jesus I did the sign of the cross and I told her in the name of Jesus I condemn you back to Hell. Then I saw the entity fade away and it said it would be back. Then I went back to bed.

"But there is something else we should talk about and that is Robert Shaw. We should research the man because we must find out what your ex-boyfriend's real name is I know it has been four years, but we should do it so that way there will be closure."

Linda was thinking about what Chris had said and one part of her did not want to believe it and another part of her wanted to believe him. At this point, she did not want to deal with this. She just wanted to move on. She wanted to forget all about this and move on with her life.

Linda said, "Listen, Chris, I appreciate you trying to help but what you are saying sounds a little far-fetched. It sounds a little crazy. I mean if we tell people this, they are going to think we are weird."

At this, Chris was fuming and he knew there was not a damn thing Linda was going to do about it. He had this funny idea that she was a non-believer in what he was saying.

"Why didn't you call Tina? What will it hurt? Get your point of view on what she thinks. She will not think you are weird or me for that matter. She can at least investigate what is going on. If you are not going to believe me, you should at least talk to Shayne, and he will not lie, and when he tells you at least it will back up my story. Why are you being so difficult?" asked Chris.

The reason Linda did not call her so-called friend Tina Garfield for granite was she could help her. But the biggest reason she would not call her was because they had a falling out. To Tina, it was not a big falling out, but Linda made it bigger than it was. So, after all these years they do not talk. Tina's name was never mentioned until eighteen years later.

Linda was getting frustrated and felt like Chris was cornering her and she did not like that feeling. She felt like a dog cornered up against the wall and when this happens what do animals do? What all animals did when they were or felt like they were being threatened was attack, and they attacked not wanting to hurt you, they did it to protect themselves.

Linda said, "I do not have time for this shit. I am not being difficult. I am not going to ask Shayne about what he saw because the only thing he is going to do is take your side like he normally does. He would not even tell me the truth even if I asked him. When you are not here if I asked the same question and if I told him to be honest, he still defends you and takes your side. When it comes to Tina, is a remarkably busy woman. She does not have the time to come to Lynn on this bullshit. Plus, she has kids, and she would not be able to get a sitter in time after Matt died. She has been a mess ever since that happened."

"FUCK!" Chris yelled.

Linda saw Chris was leaving but he stormed out of the

kitchen. Usually, when he does this, he gets angry especially when people do not believe him.

Linda said, "Where are you going?"

Chris said, "I'm going for a walk to cool down."

That would be the last time that Linda would see Chris Samuels alive again. She ignored him. She heard the baby monitor go off and heard Michelle crying. She needed her mommy. She needed either a diaper change or her bottle changed. So Linda went into the room to check on her baby. She saw Michelle and picked her up and saw that her diaper was saggy; that meant one thing she needed to get was a new diaper.

So, Linda went over to the bureau and grabbed a diaper, baby wipes, and baby powder so she could put it on Michelle after she wiped her off clean but before she put the new diaper on.

She walked over to her bed and put the baby wipes on the bed, next to that she put the white diaper, and next to that, she put the baby powder on the bed.

Then she went to get a towel which was in the closet across the room. She grabbed a shitty one. So, that way if it gets dirty, she will not care. She put the towel on the bed, it was nice and neat and then she turned around and grabbed Michelle.

She started to make funny noises to try to get Michelle to smile but she was still crying. She put her on the towel; she took her jammies and took the diaper off. She tied the diaper, and she was amazed that it was not bad. It was just pee, so she wiped her up and put the new diaper on. Before she did that, she put baby powder on and put her jammies back on. Michelle was happy she was smiling.

Linda put her back in the crib and Michelle fell back to sleep.

Linda put everything away threw out the dirty diaper, walked out of the room, and went into the kitchen to tend to the dinner she was cooking for her party tonight.

Chris was out for his walk, but this walk was going to end very quickly and that was because he was going to try to rob someone who in his eyes looked like a bitch and would be an easy target to rob but he could not be more wrong.

There was this guy who was about six feet tall, two inches tall. He worked for a living. He was working for a movie theater in Revere, Massachusetts at the time, and he had a paycheck of eight hundred dollars left over. So, he was walking up Woodman Street. He was skinny, he was walking off a meal he just had, and he was new to Lynn. No one told him never to count his money in the open in Lynn. This is called flash money and it is a fantastic way to get robbed.

He always wore his pants to his waistline. He did not like wearing clothes below his waist. He thought that was disgusting and he felt that it should be against the law.

He had blonde hair, which he had cut into a fade, he just had his eyebrows plucked and waxed. He usually does this once a month. The reason is because if he does not his eyebrows grow thick, and he grows a unibrow and it looks ugly. He has hazel blue eyes and most girls always tell them that if they are looking for a date with him, they are barking up the wrong tree because he tells them he is gay.

In most cases, women will leave it at that but yes, they

get pissed because they think he is hot. Who tried to get with him when she started to flirt with him? She was rubbing her body up against his and he told her?

"Oh, honey you are barking at the wrong tree. I did not come out of the closet to go back in." The man said.

He had a black, long-sleeved shirt tucked into his blue jeans which did not match but he did not care. When he walked, he would strut his ass and walk like a horny woman would when looking for sex.

Then he stopped and wanted to see how much money he had so he pulled out his money from his right front pocket and he had a roll of twenties, so he started counting aloud.

"Twenty... forty... sixty... eighty... one hundred... twenty... forty... sixty... eighty... two hundred... twenty... forty... sixty... eighty... three hundred... twenty... forty... sixty... eighty... four hundred."

The man put his money back in his pocket and he saw this guy who was taller than he was. He thought he was so cute. He was thinking that because he was so tall, he had a huge package. The old saying is that the taller you are the bigger the package. Chris did not care if he was gay or not. The only thing that was going through his mind was this man has four hundred dollars on him and he was going to run his pockets, but he also knew this man would give it up because he looks like a bitch. So, Chris walked up to him.

Chris said, "Hey man what's up?"

"Hey what's up?" the man said.

Chris said, "Hey what's your name?"

The man said, "My name is Michael Connor. What is yours?"

Chris said, "My name is Chris Samuels."

Michael said, "Hi Chris it's very nice to meet you?"

Both men shook hands. "Likewise."

Chris said, "So, what are you doing today?"

Michael said, "Nothing too much just going for a walk and enjoying the nice spring day. It is so beautiful out here, there is not a cloud in the sky. Cannot ask for a better day."

He was right there. Not a cloud in the sky and it felt like summer instead of spring and the weather was so warm, but it was nice.

Michael said, "Chris what are you doing today?"

Chris knew it was time to attack and go for the throat. Chris walked up to Michael in a threatening manner. He was getting scared, he was feeling like something bad was going to happen, something told him he needed to get out of there quickly. He was thinking of an excuse, but he was ready to tell Chris that he needed to go home.

Chris said, "Well, I'm looking to rob someone."

Michael smirked.

"Get that fucking smirk off your face!! Run your pockets bitch!" Chris demanded.

"What?" Michael proclaimed.

Chris was getting annoyed. "Run your pockets!"

"I do not understand. What are you trying to say?" Michael asked.

Now Chris was getting pissed. His anger was showing, his face was turning red, and he looked like a tomato. He needed to show Michael that he was serious.

Chris said, "I am robbing you. You flash and count money out in the open and I saw it, so I am taking your money so give it up, you fuck!"

Michael brought his head down and could not believe this was happening. He started to cry. He was getting nervous, he was shaking badly. He had never been told to give up his money before.

"Hey, listen it is okay you do not need to cry. It was a mistake that you made. When we make mistakes, we learn from them. Now you will learn not to flash and count your money in the open. Believe me, you are not the first in the city that flashed their money, and you will not be the last person that I have robbed. So, let us take a walk up the street. So turn around and walk with me. Okay?" Chris said.

Michael was feeling a little better about what Chris said. He understood now that he should never flush his money at Lynn because someone was going to rob him. As they were walking, they saw the police cruiser turning onto Woodman Street. Michael was thinking about flagging the police officer down so the police officer could help him and stop Chris from robbing him.

He knew that if he did that his problem would get worse. The reason he knew that was because in most cases robbery victims make a dramatic move. If they make a dramatic move, it makes the robber extremely nervous, and they will do something terrible.

When someone was robbing you, Michael learned from this lesson that it is best to give it up and then do something later.

"Now listen to this police car that is coming down the

street. What we are going to do is wave at him, so he thinks nothing is wrong. Do not even try anything and if I get any signs that you are trying to flag him down to stop me from robbing you there will be a severe problem. If you do try something I will beat the shit out of you and take your money from your pockets. Do you understand? I do not want to hurt you. I just want your money." Chris demanded.

Michael said, "I understand." I won't try anything I promise."

So, as the police car was approaching the guys waved at the police officer, and the police officer who was an older fat fuck who was stuffing his face with a white powder, a jelly-filled donut from a donut shop. He was so fat it was like he needed a donut.

It looked like he really could lose some weight. After the boys waved, the police car kept driving. Chris was looking back to see if the pig was going to turn around. In Lynn, it was always strange to see a gay person spending time together with a thug especially someone like Chris. It was very unusual, and it also meant trouble. The city had problems with thugs robbing the gay community and the reason was they did it because they were an easy target.

Chris and Michael were still walking. Woodman Street was an exceptionally long street and Chris and Michael had to find a secluded place because the houses on both sides of Woodman Street were too close to each other. Everyone was home, and they were not stupid. They would know if they saw Michael go in his pockets and give up his money to Chris, they would know that

Michael was getting robbed. The biggest thing that Chris was afraid of was that the neighbors on Woodman Street would have heard him tell Michael to run his pockets and that is because he speaks pretty, loud.

When Chris is robbing people, he gets a lot of anger when he is robbing someone. It is not because he is angry with the person, he is sticking them up because he must put the fear of God into someone to get what he wants.

"Did you see the police officer? He did not even know I was about to rob you. He waved back like nothing was wrong. Normally when a police officer sees a thug like me with a queer like you, they know that is always unwelcome news. Did you see that fat fuck stuffing his face with that jelly donut? He acted like he had never eaten before the jelly got all over his goddamn uniform? Fucking pig! You must be pissed. Shit, I would be pissed if I were getting robbed. See that path to the right?" Chris asked.

Michael said, "Yeah, I see it. What about it?"

Chris said, "That is where we are going. I cannot rob you on this street because the neighbors will call the police officers and report me for robbing you. I cannot have that."

The boys went to the path which they had to bear right and when they entered the path it was very vast with weeds everywhere.

To the left was an old factory building. It was all grey. It used to be a gun factory. The building was abandoned, and weeds were growing on all sides of the building. It was very unattractive. The city was trying to have the building demolished. They do not have the money and the residents of the neighborhood always say that someone will buy it, do something with it, and clean it out.

Michael said, "This is fucking disgusting. Does the city not care at all? They should clean it out. I am getting pricked all over the place. This is bad."

Michael was hoping to make some small talk and hopefully, he could change Chris's mind about robbing him.

Chris said, "Listen, we are not friends and I do not like you. That is why I am robbing you. Motherfucker I am done talking."

Chris was showing his anger, he pushed Michael against the building. He looked to the right to the left and to the right again to make sure no one was coming. The coast was clear. In the city, there are a lot of "Snitches" and "Rats."

Those people who report people to the police if there is a crime being committed. Chris has never been caught for robbing people, and he was not about to get caught either.

Chris saw that Michael was against the front wall of the building and he put his left hand which was twice the size of Michael's and he put a knife to his throat and started to put pressure on his throat to show fear and scare him. Michael could not move.

Chris yelled, "Now I have your ass right where I want you! There is no one to see me robbing you! I am going to go into all your pockets and run everything you have! I am going to start with your right pocket, then your left and then I am going to take your wallet! Then I am going to take your ID so if you try anything I will know where you live!"

So, Chris went into his right pocket, took the four hundred dollars out, and put it in his left pocket. Then he went back to Michael's right pocket and took his cell phone. It was one of the new ones, he put that in his left pocket as well.

Chris was scoring. He went into his right back pocket, took his wallet, and took his ID out. He put that in his left back pocket, and he put Michael's wallet back in his pocket.

Chris took his hand off his throat and backed away as Michael was catching his breath. He coughed a couple of times. "You asshole you could have killed me!"

Chris smiled. "Now remember what I said."

Chris started to walk away but what Chris did not know was Michael had a 9mm. He took it out of his left-hand pocket and down in his right-hand sock he had a silencer. He screwed the silencer on the end of the barrel of the gun. It was a perfect fit. He cocked the gun back and Michael was a good aim.

Michael yelled, "Yo, Chris I got something for your ass! You son of a bitch!"

Chris turned around facing Michael. Michael was close enough to make a headshot.

Chris said, "What?"

So, Michael took out his gun fully loaded and when Chris saw the gun, he froze. He did not know what else to do.

Chris said, "Listen, Michael, let us not get into haste. I

only wanted to teach you a lesson and rob you. So you would not make the same mistake again."

Michael's face looked stern and serious, and he had an angry and revengeful look. He was sick of people thinking they have the right to rob people and take what does not belong to them, especially people who get robbed of their hard-earned money.

Michael said, "Now you fucking listen, I work hard for my money, and I hate motherfuckers like you. You people think you have the right to rob people. Well, your luck has run out. You say you have never been caught. I am doing the police a favor by taking one thug off the street. I never understood why you people must sag your pants like that. That is the most disgusting thing I have ever seen. No one wants to see your boxers."

The gun was pointed at Chris's head and Michael was ready to shoot him. It would be a killer shot. "Got any last words?"

Chris begged for his life. "Fuck you! You can burn in hell!"

Michael laughed, which turned into a grin. "You first."

Michael pulled the trigger, and the bullet went right between Chris' eyes, and it went through the skull and lodged in his brain. There was blood coming out of the back of his head, there was blood on the ground. He had blood coming and dripping out of his mouth and he fell to the ground backwards. When his body hit the ground there was a loud thud. The blood from his head was gushing out like an oil spill. There was blood everywhere.

Michael walked over to Chris and kicked his body to make sure he was dead. Chris' eyes were wide open when he died. Michael went into his left pocket and grabbed the four hundred dollars that he stole from him, and he grabbed his cell phone as well.

He turned Chris over to his side and grabbed his ID out of his left back pocket. At first, Michael was having a tough time turning him over. It was dead weight and he put Chris on his back.

Michael put four hundred dollars in his right pocket. He put his cell phone in his left pocket. He unscrewed the silencer from his gun and by this time the silencer had cooled off. He put it in his back-left pocket, and he put the gun in his front-right pocket.

He took his wallet from his right back pocket, opened it up, put his ID in the wallet, and put it back in his right back pocket. It was starting to get dark. It was eight o'clock at night. It was time to go to Linda's party. So, Michael walked away like nothing had happened.

He started to walk outside the vast woods of the weeds and the prickles, and he was getting cut even more. He came out of Woodman Street. He saw the same police car and the same police officer driving past him and to show the police officer nothing was wrong he waved to him, and the police officer waved back. He went about his business.

He passed a couple of houses on his right before coming to 75 Woodman Street and he simply thought they were the ugliest houses he had ever seen. He thought they were homely looking. For those people, Michael knew homely meant ugly. Ugly as sin.

There was one house he did not like. He took one look at it and shook his head out of disgust. Then he proceeded and went to 75 Woodman Street. He walked up three freshly painted grey steps. He opened the blue door with a gold doorknob, and he walked in.

Michael walked up the first set of stairs and he hated the stairs. There were a lot of them, and he also hated the fact that Linda lived on the third floor. Inside the hallways were all grey including the stairs. The smell was so nice now. The apartment complex was an old building, but the property owner always kept up with maintenance on it.

So, when Michael first walked into the house, he could smell the aroma of fresh paint. He loved that smell. To him, it smelled so good. Before he went to start going up the stairs he just stood there and took in the aroma of the fresh paint odor. As he smelled the aroma of fresh paint. The aroma made him realize why the property owner was repainting the hallway. What it was like was there were holes and there was a murder in the hallway. Someone's brain was splattered all over the walls. There was a funky smell before it was cleaned and painted.

"What a smell," Michael said.

CHAPTER

EIGHT

S o, he went ahead and up the first set of stairs, he walked up. He was thinking about Chris and how she had managed it. He came to the first landing, and he stopped. He started to cry hysterically as Chris was supposed to meet up with him. This is not supposed to happen or go down like this.

He was thinking back on how he could have managed instead of shooting the guy but in Michael's mind, he felt that was the right thing to do. He was protecting himself. He did not know if Chris was going to kill him afterward. He was thinking about how he was going to tell Linda when the other thing popped up in his head. What if someone found the body and called the police?

Michael was walking down Woodman Street. He was on his way to Woodman Street for a party. He took out his money and started counting his money. Now, Chris was walking up Woodman Street. He had just gotten into an argument with

Linda, so he went for a walk. He saw a guy flashing his money. He did not know who he was, so he rolled up on him.

"Hey, what's up?" Chris said.

"Chilling you?" Michael said.

"What's your name?" Chris asked.

"My name is Michael Connor. What is yours?" Michael asked.

"My name is Chris Samuels. So, what are you doing today?" Chris asked.

"Nothing too much just going for a walk and then to a party. Yourself?" Michael asked.

"I am looking to rob someone. Run your pockets bitch!" Chris demanded.

Michael said, "Wait a minute you can't rob me."

Michael said, "The party I am going to is at 75 Woodman Street. It is Linda Carmichael's party and she invited me."

Chris was confused at first and he realized this was the gay guy that Linda asked him to protect him, meet up with him, and bring him.

Chris grinned. "Silly why did you not say so? I will bring you there."

Michael just told Chris that he knew Linda Carmichael. The reason Linda knew Michael was because he used to babysit her two boys.

Then he thought of the second scenario and this scenario takes place after Michael shot and killed Chris. One of the biggest things he was worried about was that some kids would walk by and see the body. Now and days kids have cell phones that their parents bought them to use in case of emergency.

Two kids were walking through the path where the old gun

factory was, and they were cutting down the weeds that were overgrown to the point you could not even see the path. They were the best friends. They were all in blue. They wore big baggy jeans, and their blue shirt was twice the size of them. They rocked a blue bandanna that was hanging out of the left pocket, and they were thugs. They represented. The Disciples Gang.

They just got done robbing a foreigner. They hate foreigners on North Common Street people are always getting robbed. The kids were white. Their names were Jake Kingly and James Connell.

As they were walking, they were talking about the man they had just robbed.

"Jake we fucking scored that motherfucker was loaded people should know not to cash checks in there they are so damn stupid that's why they invented banks," James said.

Jake agreed with him. "I know right but those fucking foreigners do not believe in banks. They cash their checks at a check cashing place and that is what they get. They deserve to get robbed," he said.

Both boys laughed. As they were walking, they saw a body and they looked closely and saw it was Chris Samuels. They were shocked because he was the set leader and some motherfucker killed him.

Jake said, "Someone's going to pay for this."

James knelt and started to cry.

Jake put his hand on his brother's right shoulder. "Don't worry bro, we will find out who did this, and we will kill them."

So, the boys strutted and headed to Woodman Street, and they were also going to Linda's party and what they did not know was the killer was going to be at the party. The police were never called.

That was the end of the second scenario. The last scenario that Michael was thinking about was when he went up to the third floor and he knocked on the door.

Michael goes up to the top of the third floor and he knocks three times. The knocks were very loud because he did that so Linda would hear him knocking. He wanted to make sure she heard him. She came to the door and answered it.

"Jesus! Do you have to knock that damn loud? I can hear you know! I am not senile." Linda said jokingly.

Michael said, "I'm sorry for knocking that loud but sometimes you're so busy doing other things I didn't think you were going to hear me the first time."

Linda said, "I am sorry for yelling at you." You are a little early for the party. But come on in."

So, Michael enters the party and walks through the living room. There were some people but there was not a lot. Then he walked down the long corridor and then went into the kitchen, and he sat down at the kitchen table. Linda had a few things on the stove and in the oven. She checked it out and saw that everything was good.

Michael said, "I can smell the food from the living room, and it smells so good. What are you cooking?"

Linda said, "I'm making a pork loin. I'm also making real mashed potatoes, with green beans."

Michael said, "That sounds great."

Linda walked over to the table and sat down. She took out a Newport 100 from her cigarette pack, put it in her mouth, and lit it.

"Michael, have you seen Chris Samuels?" asked Linda.

Michael said, "Who?"

"Chris Samuels," Linda said.

Michael was confused because he had no idea who this man was. He had no idea who Linda was talking about. He did not want to tell her what he had done to him. He did not want to tell her that he had killed him because he had tried to rob him. But something told him that he was going to have to tell her the truth eventually. But he wants to play it off as if he does not know him.

"I'm sorry Linda I'm not sure who you are talking about. If you could refresh my memory and tell me who he is I might be more help." Michael replied.

Linda said, "You know who Chris is?" You have heard me talk about him. I know you have. I have told you that I cannot stomach how he dresses. He likes to run into people's pockets especially when they flash their money. There was one time we were walking to the store down the street, and he saw someone flashing and counting his money.

He walked up to him and in a bit of anger he told this person to run his shit. He was in his face, and he did not do what Chris said. He got upset and he put the guy into fear and one last time he told the man to run his shit. I could not believe what he had said.

I could not believe he did that in front of me and he also did that in broad daylight. He responded that if you do not want to get robbed you should not brag about how much money you have or flash it. He said flashing it is the same as bragging that you have money. Now do you know who I am talking about?"

Michael sat back and gave a big sigh, thinking about what he was going to say next. He looked at Linda and she was leaning forward on the table. She was waiting for a response to her question. Did you see Chris Samuels? He thought long and hard about how to answer this question and he could not tell her exactly what had happened.

"Well, I know who you are talking about. I do remember you talking about him he is a funny guy. I do remember seeing him on my way up here to the party and now I think of it. I saw him on the path where the old gun shop was. It looked like he was robbing someone. He had his left hand on their throat, and he was going through their pockets. I am assuming they were flashing their money and he saw it. So, I mind my own business walking to the party. So, I do not know where he is now," Michael said.

Linda was listening to Michael talking and telling her the story. There is something that was not right with his story. What was going through her mind was if Chris were robbing someone, he would have seen Michael watching him rob this guy who was flashing his money. She knew the person could be Michael, but she could not prove that Chris robbed him.

The reason she thought that was because there was a time when Linda asked Michael to go pay Buy-A-Place for her and he decided to bring one of his so-called friends. His name was Foxx. God only knows why he was called and no one knew why.

So, they were going up Woodman Street and they cut through the path that is on the right. They were just shooting shit. So, they went into another street which was cut off, and then they would take a right and Buy-A-Place was the first building on the left on Main Street.

But before they got or were able to make it to the story, two Black men confronted them. They were well into their thirties.

CHAPTER

NINE

One man was a fat bastard. If you look at him, he looks like Fat Albert from the eighties cartoon. He was wearing all black, he was like an enforcer. An enforcer would be if one of the boys was going to rob someone, he would make them run their pockets. This man was very mean at times. He had a lengthy record ranging from burglary to assault and batteries, to unarmed robberies this man was a force to reckon with.

The other man was tall and skinny, he was a light-skinned Black man and he too wore all black he wore a heavy, black, trench coat. He was the fat man's partner in crime, and he initially did all the talking. These two guys were scumbags for what they did they scoped out on people, especially white people. The reason white people are because they know white guys will give it up without hesitation. But not in all cases.

In Michael's case, he gave them a tough time. These guys knew it. Now when the tall man robs people, he uses language that Michael is not used to.

"So, hey you guys what's up?" The tall man said.

"Nothing much what are you guys doing?" Foxx asked.

The tall man looked at Foxx and he recognized him. "I know you."

Foxx said, "Huh?"

The tall man said, "I know you."

Foxx was confused. He did not know how the tall man knew him. He could not recall. "How do you know me?"

"You know my sister? Last year you were fucking her." The tall man said.

Foxx could not believe it. "Wait a second is her name Ashlee Noble?"

The tall man grinned. "Yes, that is right. Come over here. I want to talk to you."

The tall man looked at the Fat Albert-looking man. "Keep an eye on this one. Make sure he does not move."

The tall man and Foxx walked over to the side and started to walk over to the side and have a discussion. Michael was getting a little nervous and he had to find a way to get out of the situation. But there was a fat fuck in his way.

The tall man said, "Listen we are here and the reason we stopped you two is because we are looking to rob someone and what I want to know is does your boy have any money? Tell me the truth."

Foxx sighed that he did not want to set up Michael because he liked him. He was very fond of him. Fox knew if he was to tell the tall man that Michael had money. He knew Michael would come after him, but it was a risk he was willing to take.

Foxx said, "He has a hundred dollars in his pocket."

"Okay, Foxx go about your business and get out of here," the tall man ordered.

Foxx said, "You're not going to hurt him, are you?"

The tall man laughed. "No, I am going to rob him. If he does what I tell him and gives it up, he will not get hurt."

Foxx went for a walk. The tall man was walking towards the fat man and Michael. Michael was curious about what Foxx was saying to the tall man.

"What do you think they are talking about?" Michael asked the fat man.

The fat man said, "Do not worry about what they are talking about. But do not worry you will find out very soon what they talked about because my nigga is coming to tell you and if I was you whatever he tells you to do you better do it bitch!"

So, the tall man walked over to where the fat man and Michael were. He looked at Michael and he was shaking his head.

Michael said, "What is up?" Why are you shaking your head like that?

The tall man said. "You have a bad taste when it comes to choosing your friends. You really should have chosen your friends a little wiser. Your boy just sold you out. He told me how much money you had in your pockets. Your so-called boy used to date my sister and when I saw how much of a bitch he was, so I made sure they never dated again. I fucked him up. I told any girl he tried dating that he is not a thug, he is a bitch. You are a bitch too. Look how you dress you have "rob me" written all over your forehead."

Michael said, "What is this?"

"RUN YOUR SHIT NIGGA!" The tall man said.

Michael showed no fear. Which pissed off the tall man.

"Give me your money bitch!" The tall man demanded.

So, Michael went into his pocket took out five twenties, and handed them to the man. Michael had no choice but to hand him the money. Michael knew the guy and the fat man would fuck him up. He felt it was not in his best interest to fight them he knew it was best to give up the money. He was outnumbered. The tall man put money in his pocket.

The tall man said, "Thanks for the money bitch. It was a pleasure robbing you. It was easy to rob you. I must be honest, I thought you were going to make me work for money. But in this case, you just handed the cash over without a problem. I am going to tell all my friends to rob you and I am going to tell them how easy it is to rob you."

Both men went about their business and Michael went about his.

TEN

Michael came back to reality, and he had bad images of what was happening. He remembered when he got robbed for that money that Linda gave him to pay Buy-A-Place and he mostly remembered that Foxx set him up and got him robbed and that he could remember the expression on Linda's face, and she was mad. She was hopping mad because she said Michael should have made the motherfucker work for the money. She told him that you never give up money to anyone.

He also remembered that Linda had told him that she realized that he was not from the area, and she could understand why he was scared not the fact that he got robbed. The fact that someone who he trusted, and thought it was his friend who set him up. Michael was only a trustworthy guy. He trusted everyone. He believed everything someone would tell him. He had no reason to doubt anyone. That was his downfall.

The other thing that Michael was thinking about while he was on the second platform was how he killed Chris. He felt bad doing so. After the incident when he got robbed, he swore up and down that it was not going to happen again and the fact that Chris tried to rob him upset him the most. Once again, he remembered Linda talking to him about how the city works. She felt bad that it happened.

So, he wiped his tears so when he knocked on her door, she would not see that he was crying but she was a mother, and she would know something was wrong. He walked up the stairs and started to cry again. He crawled up to the second platform. He sat up against the wall and put his head down. Michael always had ideas floating around his head. Linda has always suggested he should author a book whether it makes sense or not. She told him that he had all these crazy ideas going through his head. If he puts it on paper, he will have one hell of a book or novel.

Michael had another vision. This vision was of the future. He thought Déjà vu was ridiculous.

Michael knocked on the door three times like he normally does. It was loud to Linda. It sounded like the police or The Department of Social Services because they always pound on the door like that. She answered.

"Christ, do you have to knock like that Michael?" Linda asked.

"Sorry," Michael said as he sniffled.

Michael was crying, Linda felt bad, she wanted to know what was going on. So she asked him.

"Michael, what is wrong? You looked like you were crying. What's wrong honey?" she asked.

"Nothing," Michael said.

Linda knew something was not right. She was a mother, it was her instinct to know something was not right. She wanted to know what was going on. She was not trying to buy that. He told her that nothing was wrong.

"Come on Michael tell me what's wrong," Linda said.

"Linda, I have been having these visions and they are starting to scare me. I do not know what to do. They take place during different timelines, and I need to do something because they seem so real." Michael said.

Linda invited Michael in. Once he came into the living room, she shut the door. "I am cooking right now so follow me to the kitchen and you can tell me about it. I want to hear about these visions. So I can try to make sense of them."

So, Michael followed Linda to the kitchen, he sat at the table and sat back, he was shaking his head. He could not believe they were going to talk about this again and he also could not believe that this whole thing was happening again. He was noticeably young and the only way to solve it was to write about it.

When he was in high school, he authored a ninety-page story about what he feared, and that fear was his dream. His dreams were very vivid. They seemed so real. He used to have a pad of paper and a pencil next to his bed on his nightstand. So, if he woke up in the middle of the night, He could write about what he was thinking which had happened on more than one occasion.

Michael came back to reality, and he lifted his head, and he walked up to the third floor, and he finally got to

Linda's apartment. He knocked on the door but only once. She answered the door.

She opened the door. She was happy to see Michael. "Hey come on in."

Michael said, "Thank you I have to talk to you about something."

Linda said, "Okay let us talk in the kitchen. The party does not start for another hour I have food on the stove and in the oven to deal with."

Michael walked in and followed Linda to the kitchen. He sat at the kitchen table and Linda checked on the food and then she sat at the table.

She said, "Tell me what's going on."

Michael sighed. "Here goes nothing."

ELEVEN

Linda was curious to know about the visions that Michael was having. So, she sat down at the kitchen table, folded her hands, placed them on her lap, and was ready to hear Michael's story.

Michael began telling her the story and he was afraid she would not believe him, but he did not care.

"Well, I had visions once before but nothing like these. These scare me. They seem so damn real, but they happen at odd times, and they make me live the present, the future, and re-live the past.

"The first vision I had was in the past a little way at least it was. I was walking down Woodman Street, minding my own business and I was walking towards your house to go to the party.

"In my vision, I stopped and took some money out to count it. I saw how much I had, and I knew the reason why I did it. So, I kept walking and was at the apartment and I saw a figure walking my way. He was tall, very tall.

He wore big, baggy jeans, he wore them below his waist. He also wore an exceptionally large shirt, the shirt was large enough to cover his boxers.

"The guy saw me and walked up to it at first, I thought it was going to be a friendly conversation, so we were having a conversation. He asked me what my name was, so I told him. I asked him what his name was, and he told me it was Chris Samuels. Then we continued our conversation and like I said I did not think much of anything. There was no need to be alarmed, I did not feel like I was in danger.

"Then he asked me what I was doing. I told him I was going for a walk. I told him I had a big dinner, and I was walking it off. I asked him what he was doing, and he told me he was looking for someone to rob. Then he hit me with it. He yelled at me and told me to run with my shit. Of course, I was new to the city, and I had no idea what he was talking about. He told me what running your shit meant.

"He told me what was going to happen. He said that people who flash money or count it in the open do get robbed. He told me that I was going to go in my pockets and hand him the money and everything I had in my pockets worth of value.

"As we were walking a police officer was pulling onto Woodman Street. I saw the cruiser and I was getting ideas on how to get his attention. I was hoping to flag him down and tell the police officer that Chris Samuels was trying to rob me. But it was as if this man could read my mind, it was as if he were in my head, and he knew what I was thinking.

"He told me that I would not flag the police car. He told me if I did there was going to be trouble and he would fuck me up and then take my money and everything in my pockets. So, he told me that what we were going to do was wave at the police officer to show him that there was nothing wrong. So, as the police officer was driving by, he was stuffing his face with a powdered top, jelly-filled all over him. He was a fat fuck. When I looked closely, he was so fat his stomach was just touching the steering wheel. As we waved, he waved back.

"Chris told me that we were going to have to go somewhere else so that he could rob me because on Woodman Street the houses were too close, and he knew that people on the street would see him robbing me. He told me that they were not stupid they would know that I was getting robbed. He said that he had never been caught robbing people and he was not going to start getting caught. He looked back, and he saw the police car still driving on the street and when he saw the police officer was gone, we proceeded to go where he wanted to take me. So, we walked, and we bared to the right on a path.

"To the left of the path was a gun shop. When we entered the path, I hated it because there were weeds everywhere. It was disgusting. There were prickles everywhere as we walked through the path and the weeds got denser and denser. I saw the building was abandoned and vines and weeds were growing all around the building. I could not understand why the city did not clean up the path or do something about the building.

"So Chris pushed me up against the building. He looked to the right and then to the left and he saw that the coast was clear. He took his left hand and put it down my throat, and he put pressure on it. He was hurting me. I had a rough time breathing and then he took his right hand and went into my right pocket and took the money out and put it in his left front pocket. Then he went into my left front pocket too. Then he went into my right back pocket and took my wallet, and he opened the wallet and took my ID out and he put it in his right back pocket. Then he put my wallet back and he released his left hand from my throat and when he did that I started to cough and got my breath back.

"He told me that everyone gets robbed. He told me that this was a learning experience. It was to teach me a lesson not to flash or count my money in the open. He told me that it was not personal, it was just business. He told me the reason he took my cell phone was so that way I would not call for help. He also told me the reason he took my ID was because if I tried anything he knew where I live, and he would come to my address and fuck me up.

"He started to walk away. This is where the vision gets weird. I find myself taking my 9mm out of my left back pocket and I bent down to get the silencer and I took it out of my either right or left sock and I really cannot recall. I screwed the silencer on the end of the barrel of the gun and I told him I had something for his ass.

"He turned around and saw I was pointing the gun at him. He was trying to get out of this. He was telling me that he was just robbing me and that I should not take it seriously.

"So, I told him that he was going to pay for this, and I was sick and tired of people like him targeting people like me who work for their money. I told him I worked for my money, and I was tired of people like him taking what I worked so hard for.

"He was begging me not to shoot him. I told him that he had never been caught for robbing people and I told him today his luck was going to run out. He told me to go to Hell and I told him first, that was after I asked him if he had any last words.

"Then I fired my pistol, and I was a good shot. I shot him right between his eyes. He was bleeding like Niagara Falls from his mouth. It looked like something you see in those horror movies. His body fell backward, he was on his back.

"I walked up to him, and I went into his left front pocket and took the money and cell phone that he stole from me. I lifted his body to the side and took my ID back. I got up and left.

"I walked through the dense and vast path, and I came to Woodman Street. I was walking to your apartment, and I did not have any worries I knew that no one would find him so I walked into the front door of the apartment complex, and I walked up to the third floor.

"I banged on the door three times as if I was the police and you answered the door and asked me what to do. I need to knock that hard on the door. You invited me inside and I saw that there were some people at the party. Then I followed you to the kitchen." Michael said.

"Well Michael, you tell a relevant story. You really should author a novel. You really should pick up a pad of paper and start putting these stories on paper and type or have someone type it for you. You could make a fucking fortune," Linda replied.

Michael thought about what Linda was saying and he realized she could be right. "Would you like to hear the rest of my vision?"

Linda said, "Hold on I have to check on Michelle."

Michael said, "Okay. I will wait here."

Linda went into her room and checked on Michelle, and she saw Michelle was sleeping. She pulled the covers over up to her neck, wound up her toy, and smiled and was glad to see her daughter was well and sleeping. Michael went into Linda's son Chris's room, and he was down for a cat nap. Michael had a demonic presence to him. He was acting a bit strange. He was not acting himself. But Linda was not seeing the full picture of how Michael was acting. He was acting like there was a demonic presence in him.

He walked up to Chris. He was sleeping on his side, and he whispered in his left ear. "KILL THE BABY!"

Chris said, "How? Which baby?"

Michael said, "Take the pillow in the crib that says *Michelle Carmichael* and suffocate her until she is dead. Which baby do you say? Your baby sister that's who."

Chris was trying to figure out if this was real or a dream. But he could not tell, he was still in a dream state. One part of him did not want to kill her because he loved her but the other part of him wanted to kill her because his mother showed her all the attention, and he knew it too.

Chris said, "Why do I have to kill her?"

Michael was thinking about why. He was thinking

about how he was going to tell Chris in words he could understand because he was just a kid so he would not be able to comprehend big words or what they meant.

"She is going to save mankind from evil and we can't have that Satan does not want you must kill her and when it comes to your mother, she is having a party and there will be a lot of booze and right when it is time for her to go to bed, I will put something in her drink, so she will sleep the entire night. She will not hear you suffocating the baby. Once you do this you will be evil and do evil things. When I touch you on the shoulder you will be under my complete control. Do you understand?"

Chris said, "Yes I do."

Michael touched Chris and Michael's evil energy was going into Chris and Chris was getting lit up. He was turning blue the same color as Satan. His body was getting filled with a demonic force that was controlling his body. Chris opened his eyes just for a second. He did not turn around, he had a shit-eating grin on his face.

"Master?" Chris asked in a devilish voice.

Michael said, "Yes spawn."

Chris said, "I'm ready to serve your every need."

Michael said, "Within time once I spike your mother's drink and she passes out I will wake you up and tell you when to kill Michelle but when people consider this, they will not believe her, and it will look like the evil Linda is doing it she will be here to watch you kill Michelle and I will watch you do it as well."

Chris said, "Okay Master let me know." I am sure you command. Where are you going?"

Michael said, "Tell your mother more lies."

Chris said, "Did you kill Chris Samuels?"

CHAPTER
TWELVE

Michael had to think about it he had to be careful about what he had to say. He was concerned if he told Chris the truth, he was afraid that he was going to tell his mother and if he lies to him, he knew once the trance wore off, he would still tell his mother and if that happened he would have to kill everyone in the apartment.

Michael said, "Yes I did."

Chris said, "Good. I hate him anyway."

Michael walked out of Chris' room and went back into the kitchen. Chris turned red, he had evil in him, Michael possessed him, Chris was under his control and Chris now must do what he says.

Michael sat down at the kitchen table, and he saw Linda come out of her room before she came to the kitchen table. She stopped at the stove, shut it off, and moved the pots to one side so that she would have room for the pork loin. She shut the oven off and opened the stove. She bent down and took out the loin and as she was bending down Michael was staring at her fat, tight ass. Which is odd and that is because Michael is gay.

What was weird was that he liked it when she wore tight jeans and that was because it showed off her figure and he wanted her, he knew it would never happen. That is because every time he asked her "Do you want me?" She would always respond. "Don't flatter yourself."

The pots that were on the stove she put them on the left burners on the stove so that way she could put the pork loin on the right. She bent down and opened the oven door. She grabbed the potholders to get the loin out of the oven. The potholders were above the oven. Then she proceeded to get the pan out of the oven. Which had pork loins in it. She placed it on the right side of the stove. Perfect fit.

Then she bent down one last time to shut the oven door. Then she put the potholders back above the stove where she got them. Then she walked to the refrigerator and grabbed two cheap beers, one for her and one for him. He cracked his open and then she sat down across from Michael, and she cracked hers open. She sat back and grabbed her can and took a sip, a long sip, and Michael did the same.

Linda said, "Tell me about the next vision."

Michael said, "Well the next two visions are kind of together. The first one I'm going to tell you about is what I thought happened after I got robbed and after I shot Chris and the other one is when I was walking down Woodman Street and Chris saw me flashing my money and the beginning is the same where he talks to me showing me no fear he asks what I'm doing and I tell him the same. I am going to a party here and he tells me he is looking to rob someone, and he tells me to run my shit and I tell him the party I am going to. He asks me why I didn't tell him sooner. He shows me and brings me to the party."

Linda said, "Oh."

Michael said, "I will start with the next vision."

CHAPTER

THIRTEEN

"I was walking up the hallway stairs and I came to the first landing but as I was walking up the stairs, I was smelling the nice fresh paint. I could tell it was just painted and I loved the smell of fresh paint when I came to the first landing, and I found myself against the wall. I was thinking after I shot Chris two thugs were walking through the path, the big dense weeds of the path.

They were members of the gang The Disciples and they were coming from the check cashing place that was in the city they had just robbed an undocumented motherfucker and they scored they had a lot of cash on them and the cash they took was so easy for them to take. The boys were wearing all blue, they wore big, baggy jeans, wore their jeans below their waistlines, and wore big, baggy blue shirts that covered the jeans so that way their boxers would not show.

They both had a blue bandanna fold hanging on the outside of their left pocket and the reason for the left pocket is because The Disciples do everything on the left and they say that the left is right, and the right is wrong. When they attack, they attack in groups like a pack of vicious rabid coyotes.

So, the boys were talking about the bitch they had just robbed. One of them was telling the other he could not understand why people go to a check cashing place when cashing a check especially when the checks are a lot of money. They have a chance of getting robbed.

He could not understand why undocumented motherfuckers did not get a bank account.

The other one agreed with him, and he told him it was because they did not want to be deported back. Having a bank account, the feds can find out where they are and keep track of what they are doing.

They both agreed that robbing undocumented motherfuckers was easy and simple. When they come out of the check cashing place they always flash and count money in public and these thugs hate it when they do that. That gives them the right to stick them up and take their shit. The thugs do it all the time and that is because they know that the undocumented will not report it. After all, they are afraid that the police will find out they are in the United States illegally.

So, as they were walking through the vast dense woods, they were cutting down the weeds, so they could get through with no problem, and that way they wouldn't get caught up in the weeds when they saw that the body had a gunshot wound in the front of the head in between his eyes they recognized the victim. It was one of their leaders and they knew what they needed to do.

They swore revenge on the motherfucker who did this. With the gang, they always took the law into their own hands. They always believed that if the police got to them first, they would be lucky. Then they walked along the path and they ended up on Woodman Street. They were on their way to this party.

The next vision is about when I am walking down Woodman Street and I am on my way to the party. I found myself stopped for a minute and I was kind of curious about how much I had in my pockets so I took my money out and I started counting my money and when I was finished, I counted four hundred dollars and I put in my pocket, and I started to walk further, and I can't tell you why I was counting my money. I mean I know that is not a smart thing to do because people may see me counting and they are jealous especially people who do not have a pot to piss in so they will try to rob me. So, I saw someone walking up Woodman Street and it was Chris Samuels. The closer I got I realized it was him.

He walked up to me, and he started talking to me like most people do you know shoot the shit with you and asked me where I was going so I told him that I was going to a party. He also asked me what my name was, so I told him who I was. Then I asked him the same thing and he told me his name is Chris Samuels. Like the other vision, I asked him what he was doing, and he told me he was looking to rob someone. Then he hit me with it and he told me to run my shit.

So, I told him wait a second you are robbing me. He

told me yes and then I mentioned that the party I was going to was at 75 Woodman Street and he told me why I did not tell him that to begin with, so he walked with me and showed me where the apartment is and the party." Michael finished.

FOURTEEN

So Linda sat back and grabbed her beer and took another sip. Michael did the same telling her about these visions he had. All the talking made him thirsty. He shook his head. "Wow, talking to you is making me thirsty. By the time I am done, I am going to have another beer. This beverage is so good."

Linda said, "Wow these stories so far are so good and so intriguing you must put them on paper. They would be a blockbuster smash. You could make millions on this you could make it into a novel. Well, I must use the bathroom and then I must cut the pork. I will be right back."

Linda got up from her seat that was at the kitchen table, and she felt a little woozy from her beer. She could not understand it. She never felt like that. She started walking to the bathroom which was in the hallway on the left.

Michael looked behind his back to see if she was in the bathroom and he wanted to make sure no one was coming, and he went into his left pocket and took out a plastic bag with a white powdery substance. It was the highest Vicodin you could get and before he came over to the apartment, he crushed some and put it in a bag. He looked back and saw the coast was clear and he put half of the Vicodin in her beer, and he was hoping that it would knock her out and once it did, he could cause havoc.

Linda was coming out of the bathroom. She had no clue what Michael did, and she also did not know yet that Michael killed Chris. She was walking into the kitchen and stopped by the stove. Her back was towards Michael, and she grabbed the knife, so she could cut the pork loin and so that way people could take a piece or two. But the problem was that no one was coming over, so she was cooking for a large crowd for no reason. After she was done cutting the loin, she returned to the kitchen table.

Linda said, "Wow like I said this story is super good and you said you have another vision to share with me?"

Michael said, "I have two more to share. One takes place in the future and the other one in the past. I will tell you about the future and about the past. So I was still on the platform that was before the second set of stairs, and I was thinking about how you would react to what happened in the vision. I was coming up the stairs I came up to the third floor and I pounded on the door like I was from the Department of Social Services. So, you asked me to come in and I tried to stop crying but you saw that I was upset, and you asked me what was wrong, and I told you I was fine but you're a mother and you weren't buying it.

"So, I came in like the other visions played out together and they happened at the same time, so I walked in, and I sat at the kitchen table while you were cooking what you are cooking now. It smelled so good. The aroma was from the hallway to the kitchen.

"I sat at the kitchen table, and we started to talk so I told you the story of what happened. You asked me if I knew where Chris was and at first, I did not know who you meant, so I told you that I did not know anyone by that name. Then he told me his name was Chris Samuels and I still did not recall him. Then he began to describe to him what he looks like, what type of clothes he wears, and what you mentioned to him before. I still did not know who you were talking about. Then you were getting real upset and it showed, and you began to tell me the story about how you guys were walking to the store that was around the corner from the apartment and you continued to tell me that he saw someone flashing their money and he walked up to him in a threatening manner and told them to run their shit. You also said that you could not believe that he was robbing someone in front of you.

"Then I realized who you were talking about, and you asked me if I had seen him, and I told you a story about when I saw him. I told you I was walking down Woodman Street and I was walking, there was a path that had the old gun shop that wasn't torn down and I saw him robbing someone and I also realized that he was robbing the person because he saw them flashing their money. After I saw him robbing this person I walked away and I continued about my business when I told you that it was like you thought I was bullshitting you. What was going through your mind was I was the person he was robbing, and you had a feeling that it was true because of what happened to me before with Foxx.

"I came to reality and was hoping it was just a vision. I was hoping it was not true. So, I walked up to the second set of stairs, and I got to the last platform, and I sat down on the floor and put my head down and I was thinking about my last vision which took place before all of this, and it was then when Foxx set me up. You asked Foxx and me to go pay at Buy-A-Place, so we decided to walk up Woodman Street and we took the path, and we ended up on the street that connects the street that is adjacent to Woodman Street. Two Black men confronted us. They were wearing all black which is typical that is what Black people do rob innocent white boys that's why they are called animals and uneducated motherfucker other words they are niggers, and they are who they claim to be.

"One of them knew Foxx. He pulled him aside and he started to talk to him and the one that was guarding me was making sure I was not going anywhere. He was like my height and went over to talk to Foxx. So, the fat guy looked like Fat Albert. He was so fat he made Fat Albert look skinny yes, he was a fat fuck. But he still looked like Fat Albert from the cartoon back in the eighties. He was like an enforcer of the two and the tall one was like I said he knew him because Foxx used to date his sister until he put an end to it.

"So, Foxx without a problem told him I had one hundred dollars on me and so he told Foxx to go about his business I saw Foxx leave and the tall guy came up to me and told me that I should partake with a different company and he continued to tell me that Foxx told him that I have money in my pockets to be honest with you I wasn't trying to get killed for one-hundred dollars so I handed it to him.

"Then I came to reality for the last time, and I tried to wipe the tears off my eyes, and I came to your door, and I knocked once, and you asked me what was wrong, and I told you that I needed to talk to you about my visions and that's all my visions."

Linda sat back in her chair and could not believe what she was hearing. It was like something that came out of a movie. She grabbed her beer and started to drink the rest of it and as she was drinking it. Michael was watching her drink it and he stared at her and smiled. He began to chuckle for a bit. She did not hear him.

"Well, that is some story you need to buy some notepads and start writing this. You're a smart guy you can write in detail and when you do like I said you should type it up and send it out I'm sure it will be great." Linda said.

The Vicodin that Michael put in Linda's drink was hitting her like a ton of bricks and she was starting to pass out. It looked like what he was doing to her was working and he was waiting for her to completely pass out so that way he could make Chris kill the baby. She was feeling sleepy.

"Michael, I need to lie down. I am not feeling so hot. I do not know what it is," Linda said.

So, Linda got up and started to walk through the hall-way, so she could sleep on the couch and as she was walking through the hallway, she was grabbing on the left side of the wall to hold her balance. She barely made it to the loveseat that was in the middle of the living room against the wall. She fell on the loveseat and closed her eyes. She was out for the rest of the night.

Michael went into the living room and saw she was snoring, and he knew she was out like a light. He locked the front door, then walked down the corridor, and went into the kitchen. He started to wrap the dinner she made and put it in the refrigerator, she had a lot of room in there because she had not gone food shopping yet. Then he locked the door in the kitchen, and he saw evil Linda hovering over Michelle, she looked at Michael and smiled. Michael turned off the baby monitor in the kitchen and brought it to the room. He shut off the one in the room and he set both monitors on the windowsill near the crib.

"Go get Chris it's time to kill the baby." Evil Linda said.

The reason Michael shut both monitors off and put them in the room was that he did not want Linda to hear Chris suffocating Michelle.

"Okay, I'll wake him up and bring him in here," Michael said in an eerie voice.

So, Michael was walking through the kitchen, and he went halfway down the hallway, and he took a right into Chris's room, and he woke him up.

"Chris." He whispered.

"Yes, master," Chris said.

So, Chris got out of bed as if it was Christmas morning. He took Michael by the hand, and they took a left out of the room and went through the kitchen and took a right after the stove into his mother's room Chris opened his eyes and he saw the evil version of his mother. She was dressed all in black and he could see other demons surrounding the crib. Vetis and Valoc were there as well.

Michael kneeled facing Chris. "It's time to do what you were born to do. We are all waiting."

FIFTEEN

Chris saw other demons in the room. The most important one he saw was Evil Linda. She was an entity that had been floating around for some time and she came out when Chris's mom was stabbed for years before 73 Woodman Street. She looked at Chris and saw Michael was controlling him.

Linda looked at Chris like a mother would. She smiled. "Hey, darling you know what needs to be done."

Chris was having second thoughts about doing this, which did happen. The spell on Chris that Michael put on him was wearing off. He was shaking his head, and he did not want to do this.

"Chris, you must, or I'll have to make you do this for us." Evil Linda said.

Chris still did not want to suffocate his baby sister.

"I don't want to do this," Chris said.

Evil Linda sighed and went right into Chris, and he felt weird and that is because Linda is possessing him. He was feeling a little woozy and he was trying to fight possession and he could not resist Linda. She was an immensely powerful entity, and he was fully possessed. His eyes were as red as blood.

"Where's the pillow?" the demon asked in a deep, eerie voice.

Michael said, "I'm glad you have come to your senses and done what you are born to do spawn."

So, Chris saw the pillow in the crib. It was all white and it had her name engraved on the pillow he was hovering over Michelle, and she was sound asleep. She did not wake up once and did not wake up once and did not see it coming. He put a pillow in her face, and he knew it would not take much to kill her. Michael was smiling because he was happy with what Chris was doing and that is because Michael was not a person, he was a demon.

Chris continued to push down on the pillow and apply pressure on Michelle's face she was squirmy and tried to break free. She started to scream but no one would hear her. It was no use Chris was too strong for her as she was trying to break free Chris pushed even harder.

"DIE JUST DIE! I HATE YOU AND I DON'T WANT YOU HERE! YOU GET ALL THE ATTENTION AND IT'S NOT FAIR SHAYNE I SHOULD HAVE ALL THE ATTENTION NOT YOU BITCH! NEVER COME BACK!" Chris said in a dark and eerie voice.

Then the act was over she was dead, and he took the pillow from her face and saw she was no longer breathing, he closed her eyes and put the pillow gently on the side of the crib. He then closed her mouth and then he turned her body and put her face on the pillow to make it look like she had died from crib death.

The evil spirit that was in Chris was Linda and she was starting to come out of Chris, and it hurt him for a moment, and he came to his human senses, and he looked at Michelle and saw she was not breathing. He could not believe what he had done.

"Oh my God what have I done?!" Chris cried.

Michael said, "What you were born to do." You did good and now evil will be with you all the time. Every time you wake up and every time people look at you, they will not see this cute innocent little boy anymore. They will see evil. They may even accuse you of killing your sister and they will sense what you did but you had the help they will know that you got a little help, but people are not going to want to know that you were the one that killed your sister and that is the fact that she did not die from crib death. The police when they investigate, may say that she died from crib death, and the medical examiner may conclude in his report that is exactly what she died from. But people like clairvoyants and demonologists will know that you killed Michelle and the reason they will be able to know that is because they will be able to sense it."

Chris was confused, and he did not understand what was going on. "Sense it? Had help? What do you mean?"

Michael said, "Let me explain something to you." People will be able to sense that you are evil, and they will not want to be able to hang out with you. People will fear you because you can kill a human being. The reason you had help was because the spell I put on you was wearing off and you were having second thoughts about suffocating your sister so the evil entity that took the form of your mother gave you a little help. Get a brief time. She possessed you to get what we wanted you to do and believe me it was a necessary act to do and if she did not your baby sister would have lived. We cannot have that. I do not think I have to explain the other question that you had. You get it now."

Chris was still a little confused. Chris needed to get to bed before his mother woke up from the deep sleep that Michael put her in after he spiked her drink and that was a necessary thing to do. He could get that close to Michelle, and he used her oldest son to commit the perfect murder.

"I need to get to bed before my mom wakes up and makes coffee and checks on the baby and when she finds out that the baby is dead, she is going to freak out and I'll wake up and deal with it," Chris replied.

Michael said, "I'll take you to your room and put you to bed."

Michael walked over to the windowsill, grabbed one of the baby monitors, and turned it on. He also turned on the one that was on the windowsill that Linda put there.

Chris and Michael were walking out of the bedroom and Chris left the room first Michael was behind him, and she shut the door very slowly acting as if Michelle was sleeping. He looked back and saw the demons fading away one by one. He looked at Linda.

"See you soon," Linda said in a dark voice.

Then she faded away. Michael put the other baby monitor on the kitchen table in the same spot that Linda had it. Next to the monitor, Michael placed an obituary notice. It was his.

Then they went down the hallway and took a sharp right to Chris's room. Chris jumped into bed and Michael looked at him and wished him a good night's sleep. Michael knew he was going to need it.

Chris lay down by his side. "I'll see you soon."

Michael said, "You can count on it kiddo."

So, Chris fell fast asleep and was in the same position when Michael woke him up to suffocate Michelle. What Chris did not see was Michael fading away. He was a demon that wanted to cause havoc and pain to others, and he completed his mission.

CHAPTER

SIXTEEN

Linda slept the entire night. Now normally she (like clockwork) got up in the middle of the night to go to the bathroom. But that night she did not.

So, she got up and sat straight up. Her back was cracking. She could hear the bones cracking and she was feeling the pain as well. It hurt her and that was because a few years back she fell down a flight of stairs in her doctor's office. That was the reason her back always hurt.

Linda had this guy staying with her. He was her boyfriend and when he saw her hunched over in agony that day in the kitchen, he told her to stop faking.

So quickly Linda came home from the hospital after she fell down a flight of stairs. She was in agony. You could tell she was in agony. Before she fell down the stairs, she injured herself in a car accident.

Linda's boyfriend's name was Joe Groin. Every time someone complained about their groin, or they even saw the word groin and if he heard it, he informed people not to call him, even though that was his last name which happened to be what guys refer to their balls. Joe was a younger version of an old gangster in a mafia movie.

So one day Linda's back went out while she was in the kitchen cooking dinner. Joe saw Linda bent over in agony. He started to smirk.

"Is there something funny asshole?" Linda exclaimed as she gave Joe a dead stare. It hurt her to do that. Joe was at the point where he thought it was funny but at the same time, he was thinking Linda was full of it.

Joe had this stupid fucking look, and he had a bad habit of putting his hand in Linda's face.

Joe said, "You're fake it!"

Linda was furious. "Fuck you, Joe!" She yelled.

Joe said, "You are only saying that because you are looking for attention." You want people to feel sorry for you."

About a month later, she fell down a flight of stairs but only this time when she came back home, she had the X-rays that the hospital gave her. She walked into the apartment and slammed the door. She made a book line to the kitchen. She could see Joe in the kitchen talking and laughing and making racial jokes to one of his friends. Linda saw Joe in the chair to the right of the kitchen table.

"I'm faking it, huh?!" Linda yelled.

Linda threw the X-rays in front of him. His company laughed at him, and Joe was so embarrassed that his face turned as red as a tomato.

"You got something to say now?! I am faking it huh, motherfucker?" Linda yelled.

Joe grabbed the manilla envelope and opened it and it was Linda's X-rays of her back.

He put it up to the light. He saw the damage to her back and that is when he knew she was not faking it.

Joe looked at Linda and he was ready to open his mouth to apologize to Linda. But when she saw his mouth open, she thought he was going to say some smart-ass remark.

"Nope. Do not bother I know you are going to say something smart or dumb."

Joe gave her that famous stupid look he always gave her. Linda ignored Joe and did not even look at him and that was because she knew she had won. She was victorious. Then she walked away.

Linda came back on April 20, 1999. She started to stretch her arms in the air acting like she was reaching for something. Her hair was all over the place.

So, she got up and noticed that everything was quiet. Shayne and Chris were both sleeping so she figured they would be up first.

She was a little tired and she walked down the hallway and went into the kitchen. She was getting her motherly instincts and it told her something seemed out of place.

So, she went into the pantry, and she started to brew coffee. When she was done, she knew her two boys were sleeping. Normally Michelle cries for her momma. It was quiet in the apartment and you could hear a pin drop. She went into her room to check on her baby and when she went in Michelle was lifeless. She went closer and checked for a pulse and she knew something was wrong. She knew her baby was dead.

Linda could not believe what she had seen. She started to burst into tears. Her eyes were extremely watery. Her tears were coming down like Niagara Falls.

She had her right hand over her mouth. She did not want to wake up her kids. She walked out of the room and closed the door. She did not want her to see that their baby sister was gone. She does not even know how she is going to tell her kids.

Linda walked over to the kitchen table and something caught her eye. It was a piece of paper perfectly flat on the table next to the baby monitor. She walked over, and she got a closer look at it. It was an obituary notice.

When she saw the obituary notice when she saw the picture of the name. She was in shock. It was Michael Connor, the same Michael who was talking to her and the one who was telling her about the visions he had of what happened to Chris Samuels. She just realized then and only then that Michael was a spirit but not a good one. She freaked.

When she read the obituary at first, she could not figure out how she died and at first, she thought it was a gag that one of her kids was playing on her. That is a sick joke to play on someone.

As she was reading the obituary, she saw how he died, and it was a fatal car accident. A drunk driver had hit him head-on. Michael died instantly.

She could not believe that this was happening. This whole time she was talking to a ghost or spirit. But no, it was worse, she was talking to a demonic entity and she did not even know that. She was floored.

She screamed.

Chris and Shayne heard their mother screaming. They both came out of their rooms and ran to Linda to figure out what was going on. The boys hugged their mother.

Chris said, "Momma what's wrong?"

Shayne just looked at his mother with a quizzed look. When this happened, he was too young to understand. Shayne knew there was something wrong. He could sense it. When he saw his mother crying, he knew she was hurting but he did not know why.

Chris knew something was wrong, so he continued his questioning.

"Momma, what is wrong? Why are you crying? It is okay momma you can tell me." Chris comforted his mother. Linda had no way of knowing how she was going to tell her boys what had happened.

Linda eventually told her kids what had happened, and she called the police. The police came. At first, they held Linda at bay and started to accuse her of killing her baby. Then the detective was the same detective who was there when she got stabbed. He sent the police officer who accused her of killing her baby off the case. Then he apologized to Linda. The police came, and they did an investigation.

They concluded that the death of Michelle Carmichael was unknown. When Linda told them about Michael Connor, she told them she was talking to a ghost. They thought she was nuts. They thought she was ape-shit crazy. So, they agreed with her because she was grieving.

The medical examiner and the police were there for hours. A detective was taking fingerprints. To his surprise there were none.

So, Michael Connor was to the side looking in and he saw how miserable Linda was and he started to laugh at her. This is what demons make laugh at people who are good and are trying to do the right thing. But when something happens especially a mother trying to deal with the death of a child the demons find that very funny because they think they have won. Then Michael faded away.

Linda heard a demon laugh. She could hear him laughing at her and yelling at what she was going through and yelling at it. That right there is when she needs to move. So, she moved here and there. The times she did move she did not have any more problems with spirits and demons.

SEVENTEEN

Linda was very frantic, and the two boys woke up that morning, the morning of April 20, 1999. They were wondering what happened and Linda had to tell them that their little sister was dead. The boys cried, especially Shayne. Chris could have cared less. But what got them was that Michael Connor was dead, he was a demon. Linda had reason to believe in some way or form that he had something to do with this.

The police did their investigation and of course, it was not the same police officers that investigated her stabbing but they were smart as they brought her through the ringer. They accused her of killing her baby but after carefully investigating they concluded that Michelle Carmichael died of crib death. That is what the medical examiner ruled it as.

Linda knew there was something wrong with the apartment. She knew she had to get out of the apartment, and she also knew if she did not the evil spirits would go after her two boys and eventually come after her, so she was not taking that chance. She saw a three-bedroom in Salem. She went over there to look at it when the boys were in school, and she liked it very much. She put the deposit down on it immediately. Everything had been redone and she thought it would be perfect for her.

So, when she left and went back to Woodman Street, she told the boys, and they moved to Salem. In the year two thousand, they moved to 529 Boston Street in Salem; she was on the third floor. She had to hire movers to help her with her stuff but once they got the stuff in the apartment, she was happy. She was thinking now I can live a normal life without that evil following me everywhere.

In two-thousand and three, she got a roommate whose name is Nicholas Connors. He works at a movie theater in Danvers and some days he likes his job, other times he cannot stand it. He is a supervisor and he enjoys his position. A year before he moved in Linda once again faced another tragedy and that was the death of Chris her oldest son. Which occurred on October 31, 2009.

He was in a car with some friends they were racing and the driver lost control of the car and he crashed head-on into a tree. A couple of seconds later the car exploded, and the driver of the car was Nicholas Connors the same Nicholas Connors who was living with her, but she didn't know it yet.

So, after he died, she put an ad in the paper saying she was looking for a roommate and Nicholas answered the ad. He came over and looked at the room and the area where he would spend most of his time sleeping and he agreed to move in. The Carmichaels had been free of anything demonic since 1999.

But nothing prepared this family for what was about to happen. The evil that Linda had gone well they were not done with her yet. It was not going to be the same demon, but this one would be much worse and would not be easy to get rid of.

EIGHTEEN

Nicholas Connors was on the bus, and it started to sprinkle outside. He was a tall man, with short brown hair, and hazel-blue eyes. These were so beautiful the girls would go gaga over him. He had a good skin complexion and an average-sized head. His nose wasn't too big or too small, it was simply perfect.

He worked at a movie theater that was next to the town called Danbury. He had had a long day. His uniform consisted of a white dress shirt, a tie, a black vest with his name badge on the right, black slacks, and a pair of black shoes. The word supervisor and part of his job was to train all the new folks. The theater was crowded being Halloween all over. The bus didn't take long to bring him to his destination. But when he was on the bus waiting for his stop, he was thinking about what the landlord told him about the murder that happened thirty years ago. He quickly got rid of that thought. He thought that was bullshit anyway. He yanked on the yellow cord to signal the bus stop, and he wanted to get off.

The bus stopped, and he saw the night was dark and it was starting to storm badly. The rain was coming down hard and the wind was picking up not a good combination.

"Oh, Shit!" Nicholas said as he was getting off the bus.

The bus closed its doors and drove away. Nicholas sighed. He knew even though his home was only five minutes from the bus stop, he knew he was going to get drenched from the rain and he also knew he had to walk fast in a sprint to run phase if he was going to try to dodge those raindrops.

It was a dark and stormy night; it wasn't supposed to rain. The weather forecaster was wrong as usual but it was New England. The old saying was "Wait five minutes and the weather will change".

Nicholas had a long day at the movie theater where he worked. This day he had to train a lot of people all day. He was exhausted.

When he got off the bus though his apartment was five minutes away, but it seemed longer it was like he had to go through a long tunnel and it felt like when he entered the tunnel it kept getting longer and longer before he reached the end. He hates that feeling as he was thinking about that in his head he was getting soaked, the rain was coming down like buckets. The wind was so strong it was forcing the rain to go sideways to the left and then to the right.

As he was walking fast, he passed a donut shop on the left which was closed. When this place was happening it was always crowded with all sorts of people and most police officers were in there sipping on their coffee and stuffing their faces with jelly-filled donuts. They wore slobs so the jelly wouldn't drip all over their uniforms and some of them wouldn't even notice it. It was called Donuts, Inc.

Across the street was a pharmacy. It was so large the building took up half the parking lot. They sold everything you could imagine except tobacco products because they were a pharmacy and in the state of Massachusetts it was against the law to sell it. When you walked in, there was always someone there to greet you and when you left, the same person would ask you to come again. Very welcoming. They were a family pharmacy and they have been there for years. The name was Gerald's Pharmacy.

He came to the address. It was 666 Boston Street, Salem, Massachusetts. The building had six apartments.

From the outside the building was all brick, it was pretty tall it reminded Nicholas of the original Ghostbusters movie; it was dark and creepy. The only thing it didn't have were the gargoyles on the top of the building looking down. Nicholas was glad because he felt those things freak him out even though they were made from stone. In his mind, one day they would come back to life and hurt him.

The first floor had two one-bedroom apartments both across from each other but before the apartments were six rusted old grey mailboxes. The only people who had the keys to those boxes were the tenants, the mail carrier, and the landlord. They were rusty from wear and tear and the landlord didn't care enough to get them fixed. All she cared about was when she was getting her rent.

When you go up the brown stairs which at times creaked two apartments had two, two-bedroom apartments. Most everything in this complex is brown and Nicholas was always curious why that was. It was either the landlord's favorite color or she must have gotten it cheap.

Finally, the third floor had two, three-bedroom apartments. They were two but there's a room they could be turned into a bedroom. Nicholas had one of the apartments on the third floor. It was his apartment it was his friend's apartment her name is Linda Carmichael.

Nicholas opened the dirty brown stained door that creaked every time you opened it and it freaked him out. What got him scared was all the hallway lights that were out. He was trying to feel for the railing on the left side. It was dark. He was starting to feel like a blind person. He couldn't see a damn thing.

The stairs were stained a mahogany brown color, and the hallway had a disgusting musty smell. They were going up the stairs and the stairs were so bad he could hear this annoying sound.

"Creak!"

Every step he took he could hear that sound, so he needed to get to the third floor quickly, so he started to skip steps. Then as he was reaching the second floor, he felt like someone or something was watching him. He felt eyes on him. Then he could hear the pitter-patter like another pair of footsteps were walking up the stairs. Nicholas stopped in his tracks and took his cell phone out of his front right vest pocket. He turned it on. It took a minute, and he could hear the pitter-patter again, but they were getting closer, and closer, and closer. He turned on the flashlight and shined it down on the stairs. There was nothing. Then he pointed it up the stairs and there was nothing. So he continued.

Then in an eerie, muffled voice, he thought he had heard someone call his name.

"Nicholas." The eerie voice said.

He ignored it, so he continued up to the third floor. He had goosebumps all over his body, he felt a little chill over his body, he felt a little chill, his short brown hair was sticking up from feeling fear. He got to the apartment.

Nicholas opened the door, and his roommate was playing cards by herself. She always played cards by herself. She was a little heavy-set and smoked like a chimney. She always had a cigarette in her mouth. She was in her late fifties; she always dyed her hair black. That's because it's Halloween. Boy, did she complain? She complained from the time she got up till she went to bed. Yes, she is lazy.

He saw how Nicholas looked. She had a strange look on her face.

"Hard day at work Nick?" she asked.

"You can say that. He replied.

"You are okay? You look like you've seen a ghost." She spoke.

Nicholas said, "Don't ask. I'm tired and I just want to sleep. I'm going to sleep in your son's old room."

"Good night then." She spoke.

So, Nicholas went into her twenty-eight-year-old

son's room which was adjacent to the kitchen, and he was a sports fanatic. He had posters of all the New England teams. He was ready to fall on the bed.

But there was something in the air that didn't seem right. He could smell rotten eggs in the room. He thought his roommate was cooking eggs. She's a lousy cook. She couldn't even boil water. Then he took another whiff, and he realized it smelled more like a rotting corpse. He ignored it.

Usually when there is a smell in a room, and it smells like something is rotting that usually means there is something demonic around. But he didn't believe in shit like that. He fell on the bed; he fell face first and two seconds later he was sound asleep. The room was completely dark, with no lights on, and the door was ajar. The door of the bedroom was starting to shut on its own as if someone were pulling the door shut.

CHAPTER
NINETEEN

Linda was still playing cards she was playing solitaire on her ugly poke dot tablecloth. She got it cheap she was a cheap skate.

Her kitchen had a lot of space, the walls were all white. It was white wallpaper. It was so white if you look at it from a distance you swear it's been painted. The ceiling had a fresh coat of white paint. You can still smell the paint when you walk into the kitchen.

Across from her kids' room was her room and boy was it a mess. When you walk into her room her bed is in the middle of the room and it's never made it's always a mess. Behind the bed is a brown headboard. It was a half-circle shape. Above the headboard is a window made from plexiglass. It was sealed for the winter. Curtains were covering the window, which is because Linda liked her room dark when she went to bed.

Across her bed was an oak, four-foot bureau which had six drawers. On top of that was a twenty-four-inch plasma smart television. To the left of the television is a grey DVR cable box.

On the left of her bed is a closet that has white-painted doors and shutters. The closet was large. She could fit all her clothes and some she had a shelf where she could put... well you know girl stuff and shit.

On the right side of her bed was a desk; up against the lime green wall the desk was pure oak. It was so heavy it took four people to bring it up for her. Above the desk was an oval-shaped mirror. There was nothing on the desk. There were two drawers on the left and one on the right. The rug in the room was a dark red color. It was as dark as blood. It didn't match the room.

Next to the bedroom was the living room, which wasn't too big, it was smaller than a normal size living room. There was a tan loveseat that was against the back of the white wall. The walls in the room were painted white not to mark on them.

In front of the loveseat is an oak table with oval-shaped glass over the oval-shaped table. Across the table was a wooden rectangle table also stained brown and on top of it was a nineteen-inch flat-screen television and to the right was a bunch of DVDs stacked neatly that was only collecting dust. Linda was, so she couldn't even afford a DVD player she only had enough to pay her monthly rent that's why Nicholas was there to help her with the rent and the bills. On the left of the threshold is a circular knob that turns on and off the lights in the room. If you leave it's on your left but if you enter the room, it's on your right.

Behind the kitchen table is a silver sink with a faucet

where the comes out that was silver too and it has two knobs one on the left it's crystal and in red lettering it has a capital "H" for hot, on the right there is another crystal knob and in blue lettering, it has a capital "C" for cold. To the right of the sink is a black strainer. Nicholas usually does the dishes and rinses them, especially cups. It tasted like dishwater yuck!

Next to the sink to the left is an electric stove so her entire apartment is all electric. It was white with black square burners which are a pain in the ass to clean. She never cleaned. Usually, Nicholas soaks them because she is usually too lazy to clean them, and they are filled with food caked on them.

Linda was still playing cards at the kitchen table. She suddenly stopped. She put her Newport 100 cigarette out in her black ashtray that was to the right of her. She heard her bathroom door creak open. Then she heard an eerie child's voice that startled her.

"Linda... Linda... Come play with me... I need someone to play with me... he won't let me play." The child said.

Linda was feeling goosebumps all over her body she started to shiver she slowly got up and went to shut the lights off the switch was next to the stove she flicked the switch down to shut the lights off that was above the kitchen table then she slowly walked over to the light switch by the apartment door which is on the right side she was walking backward and staring at the bathroom she flicked off the other lights now it's nice and dark so that way she could see the ghost.

She took out her phone and put the flashlight on which was in the front pocket of her blue Levi's. She walked slowly towards the bathroom, but she wouldn't go beyond the kitchen table she toed and flashed the phone's light over at the door of the bathroom.

As the light shined in the bathroom the door opened all the way.

"What the fuck?" she proclaimed.

Then she saw the head of what looked like a little boy. He had short brown hair, his eyes were bloodshot red, he was wearing a plain blue tee shirt and a pair of old rugged blue jeans and he started walking out of the bathroom.

Linda couldn't believe what she was seeing she couldn't take a video of this because her camera lens was cracked but she knew she had to call someone she has a friend who knows what to do in this case she thought she could communicate with it before she called her friend Tina Garfield. The spirit was walking slowly like a zombie towards her kid's room.

"Hey, who are you?" Linda asked.

The spirit looked at her and he started to growl. He didn't want her there, going to call her friend, he also knew what she was thinking before she was going to do it. He knew she was going to call her friend to cast him out and he didn't like that.

He said, "I'm not here for you, bitch! I'm here for your roommate. My name is Rodney Marks and I died in that room when I was twelve years old. That is my room. Your roommate doesn't belong here or sleeps in my room.

Linda was frightened. She could feel her stomach going into knots, she couldn't believe she was talking to a spirit.

"What do you want?" Linda asked.

Rodney didn't answer. He hated repeating himself, he just told her why he was here and what he wanted with Nicholas. It doesn't matter. Rodney will get what he wants that's because he's a demon.

He walked over to the room. The back of his head was facing Linda. She could see a bullet wound on the back of his head. It was a substantial size wound and she noticed green ooze dripping from his wound. It was dripping down the wound, dripping down his back and onto her floor.

Rodney walked into the room and turned around and gave Linda an evil grin then he widened his mouth. Inside his mouth, his ugly, disgusting rotting teeth were showing. Then he shut the door. Linda screamed.

She turned around and went into her room, slammed the door, sat on her bed, took a deep breath, and sighed. Suddenly there was this white light that lit up her entire room. It was a grown woman. She was all in white, and she smiled at Linda.

Linda said, "Wow you are so beautiful. Are you an angel?

The woman nodded yes. She sat next to Linda and hugged her.

"Everything will be all right. I'm going to help you. I know what's been going on with you. Please don't be frightened. I'm not here to harm you." The woman whispered to Linda.

Linda said, "What's going on here?" Why are you in my apartment? What happened to you and the little boy?"

My woman said, "My name is Maggie Marks and the little boy you saw is my son Rodney my husband his father murdered us on Halloween thirty years ago, a demon took control of my son's soul and enslaved him. You need to call your friend immediately to save his soul and your roommate's he is in grave danger. Oh, no I can feel my husband's evil presence I have to go remember what I said."

The woman vanished as if she was never there.

At first, Linda was jogging something in her mind. Linda was curious how Maggie knew certain things about her. Then she realized Maggie was a spirit. An angel to boot.

Then just before Linda was going to call Tina, she heard someone in the kitchen, but she heard heavy footsteps. It sounded like the footsteps of a man lurking around. She slowly opened the door and she saw a tall man wearing all black even though his hair was black. He looked like the demon from those exorcism films. But the only difference was that this man had a chunk of his head that was from the back and there was blood dripping everywhere. Tina's number rang twice and Tina answered.

"Hello," Tina said.

"Hi, Tina it's Linda. Can you come over? It's important," Linda said.

"Linda it's late," Tina said. "What's wrong?"

Linda said, "I know it's late but I'll tell you when you get here. I'm really scared."

Tina said, "Okay I'm on my way don't move."

Linda said, "Okay when you get here don't knock. Call me when you get here."

Tina said, "Okay no problem. I'll bring my Ouija board."

"Good, we'll need it. Bring some stuff to cleanse my apartment." Linda said.

"Oh, you mean Sage?" Tina asked.

"Yeah, that stuff," Linda said.

Tina said, "Ok I'll bring some. See you soon."

Linda said, "See you."

Both Linda and Tina hung up.

The rain slowed down and ten minutes later it completely stopped. It's eleven thirty in the evening. Linda is patiently waiting for Tina's call.

CHAPTER

TWENTY

Tina Garfield had long reddish hair and her hair strings were very thin. As thin as the string you use to thread clothes. She had an oval-shaped head, her eyes were chestnut brown, and her nose was like a beak, from a cow, people used to refer to her as a crow woman. She was very slim and had a nice figure. She was very slim and had a nice figure. She was wearing a long-sleeved shirt, tight blue Jordache jeans, and black high heels.

Tina only lives five minutes up the street from Linda. She was walking down Boston Street and she could smell and feel the dampness in the air. There were leaves everywhere blowing in every direction. People were going nuts which happened on Halloween night.

A lot of things were going through Tina's head. She had her black nap sack which had her Ouija board and the tools she needed to do a cleansing. At this time as she was drawing near the apartment, she was hoping it wasn't going to be what she feared. That was a demonic entity that was taking the form of a child. If she is right this entity is immensely powerful very malevolent and extremely hateful. She came to Linda's building.

She opened the door and noticed the hallway was pitch black, there was no light, and this typically meant evil spirits were lurking.

She took out her Android phone that was tucked in her left front pocket. Her jeans were so tight it took a minute for her to get her phone out. She put the flashlight on and proceeded to the stairs. Unlike Linda and Nicholas she wasn't scared that easily as she was walking up the first set of stairs, she could hear the stairs creak.

"Creak!"

She ignored it, she continued up the stairs and a few minutes after she could hear the pitter-patter, she could hear someone walking up the stairs. When she got to the first landing she turned around and flashed the light down the stairs and there was nothing there. She continued to the second floor.

She could smell a foul odor. The odor was so strong she had to cover her nose. It was like rotting flesh or when eggs spoil it was an odor, she was familiar with the odor. She continued to walk up the stairs and the footsteps were getting closer and closer. Now she could feel eyes on her as if someone was watching her. She needed to get to Linda's apartment and get there quickly.

She got to the second platform, and she started to walk up to the third set of stairs, and she could see Linda's apartment door. On the door, it read: 3A. The foul odor was getting stronger and stronger. It got to the point that as she was climbing the stairs, she started to cough violently, and she started to gag as if she was going to vomit. Her face was red as an apple from coughing so hard. She got to Linda's door, and she dialed her cell phone number, and it was ringing. It rang twice, and Linda answered.

"Hello," Linda said.

"Hello Linda, it's Tina. I'm at your door." Tina said.

"Give me a minute," Linda replied.

Both parties hung up and the call ended.

Linda got off her bed and her body was trembling out of fear. She opened her bedroom door and slowly walked over to the door to her apartment. She opened the door very slowly and she was overjoyed to see Tina.

Tina said, "Linda you look like you saw a ghost."

Linda chuckled sarcastically. "Very funny come in."

Tina walked in when she stepped on the cobblestone kitchen floor. She could sense an evil presence it was something demonic. She also noticed the green ooze that was in the doorway of her son's bedroom and the red blood near the sink and there was a trail of blood leading to the bedroom. Tina was puzzled.

Tina said, "Why don't you tell me what you saw?"

Linda said, "Okay let's sit at the kitchen table. I'll go over to the stove and turn on the lights above the kitchen table."

Linda went over to the light switch that was next to the stove and turned on the lights, so they could talk about what's been going on. Linda went to the table and sat in her regular seat while Tina sat across from her.

Linda took a cigarette out of her pack and lit it. Tina was eager to know.

Tina said, "Okay Linda now tell me what you saw so I have a better understanding of what's going on here."

Linda inhaled her cigarette and blew the smoke out.

Linda said, "Okay I was sitting right here, and I was playing cards." Something distracted me so I stopped what I was doing and I heard the bathroom door creak open and a few minutes later the door opened all the way and I saw this little boy coming out of the bathroom and he started to talk to me so I acknowledged him I asked who he was and he told me his name is Rodney Marks he told me he died in the bedroom when he was twelve and that is his room and he wasn't here for me he was here for my roommate.

"I got up and turned the lights off above the kitchen table and I proceeded to walk backward to shut the main light off in the kitchen. I turned on the flashlight on my phone and the back of his head was turned to me. I noticed a bullet wound and then I saw green ooze coming dripping down his back from the wound and onto my floor. He turned around and gave me an evil shit-eating grin and then he widened his smile, and I could see his rotting teeth. I screamed, and he shut the door.

"I walked slowly to my room, slammed my door, and sat on my bed and a few minutes later there was this light that shined in my room, it was so bright I knew it had to be an angel, one of the good guys. It was a grown woman. She was dressed all in white she looked so beautiful, and she sat down next to me. We started talking she was telling me her name was Maggie Marks and that little boy

I saw was her son Rodney and she continued to tell me that thirty years ago, her husband on Halloween night murdered her and her son and he shot himself in this apartment. She also told me that her son was being enslaved by a demon. She told me to call you for help and she had to cut it short because she could feel an evil presence and that was her husband. Then she vanished like she was not there. She did ask me to help her son free his soul and vanquish the demon that was enslaving him.

"I was about to call you and I heard these heavy footsteps in the kitchen, and I knew they weren't from a child, I knew they were from an adult. So, I slowly opened my door to see who it was, and it was Rodney's father. He was wearing all black, he looked like the demon in a horror movie from the nineteen-nineties except a chunk of his head was missing. He was sniffling around, and I knew he could smell me, but he didn't see me, and he was dripping blood everywhere leading a trail to my son's bedroom. He walked in. After that, I had enough and that's when I called you."

Tina knew what had been going on. She had seen the same spirits when she walked past this apartment building. She knew she had to act fast. Tina got up from her chair and started to look around, as Linda put her cigarette out in the ashtray.

Tina said, "Linda, now I need to look around. Do you mind if I look around the apartment and look at the other rooms so I can narrow it down to one room?"

"Sure, just to let you know that thing came out of the bathroom and went into Shayne's room."

Shayne Carmichael was twenty-eight years old, at the

time was sleeping over at a girlfriend's house. Halloween for her was a scary time and he was there so the boogeyman wouldn't get her. She was a scary cat. She was afraid of her own shadow.

Tina said, "Okay but listen I want you to walk with me I'm going to light two white candles one for me and one for you I'm going to shut off all the lights and we're going to walk into each room and see what we have here."

Tina lit both candles and Linda shut all the lights off. She first shut the lights off in the bathroom. Then she came back to the kitchen.

Tina said, "Are you ready?"

Linda said, "As ready as I'll ever be let's do this and get this son of a bitch!"

Tina said, "Let's begin our journey."

Tina shut off the kitchen lights. The whole apartment went pitch black. The only thing you could see was the flickering of the candles.

Tina said, "If you see something stay calm and show no fear."

TWENTY-ONE

"Why are the candles flickering?" asked Linda. Tina smiled. "That's how you know there is something demonic in the house. Entities don't like light and they are not happy we are here, especially me."

"Why?" Tina asked.

"Well, it's because I'm a very special person and I can sense evil spirits before anyone else can," Tina said.

"You're a white light?" Linda asked.

Tina laughed. "No, I'm not a witch. I'm a demonologist and a clairvoyant."

Linda shrugged and they both started the walk around. The first room they walked into was Linda's bedroom. As they walked in Linda was starting to get the heebie-jeebies, she could feel the fear going through her body, and then she started to get the shivers Tina could sense her fear. Tina turned around to face Linda. They were both standing on the side of the bed.

"Linda shows no fear. I can sense your fear. If you show fear, the entity can gain power over you and weaken you. You need to know the three stages of possession. Here they are:

- Oppression: That's when the demon and the entity make contact. You'll hear whispering, pitter-patter, moving objects. That's them telling you they are there.
- Infestation: That's the smell. The smell is like rotting eggs, rotting flesh imagines the flesh coming off the bones. You will start to see bruising on the body, and this is how they are weakening their victims. The weaker the victim, the easier it is for them to possess their victims.
- Possession: This stage is the most dangerous stage of all three stages. It doesn't just affect the victim but the loved ones or people they care about. The entity's main objective is to cause and inflict pain on others. Don't show the entity that you are afraid of it."

Tina didn't see or feel anything in the bedroom, so they moved on to the living room and when they walked in Linda could feel that someone or something was watching them. Linda turned slightly to her left and she could see these dark eyes just watching her move. Then she turned straight forward and ignored what she felt. She remembered what Tina told her about showing fear.

Tina and Linda started to walk around the living room

Tina closed her eyes she did this to see if there were any spirits besides the entity, she put herself in a trance and her outer body came out we call this astral projection which is when someone can leave their physical body. The body is only a vessel without the spirit, it's just a vessel and it's not alive.

Tina's spirit saw herself standing in front of the television with her eyes closed and Linda standing behind her. Tina saw a little girl playing with Barbie and Tina walked over to her and knelt next to her and saw she was filled with a white aurora. It was so bright, it lit the entire room. She was wearing a pure white dress. It was the same dress that she wore to her funeral. Tina touched the little girl on her shoulder and the little girl turned around and smiled at Tina.

"Hello," she said. "What's your name?"

Tina said, "My name is Tina. What's yours?"

Tina smiled back, and she couldn't believe how bright this little girl was. "You know who I am... I'm Michelle. Linda, my mother. I died of SIDS." Michelle said.

Tina thought for a moment. She realized who the little girl was, and she started to cry. She put her hands covering her face and she just cried and cried very loudly.

Michelle tapped on her right shoulder. "Tina, what's wrong why are you crying? You didn't do anything wrong."

Tina looked at Michelle. "I should have known it was you. I'm crying because I wasn't able to go to your funeral. After all, I was busy with work and everything else. Michelle, I am so sorry that I wasn't there. I can only hope you can forgive me."

Michelle said, "It's okay but you don't need to apologize to me. I know you couldn't make it you have a job and a family to look after, and I know hard after Matt died."

Tina wasn't surprised that she knew about Matt's passing. Two years prior Matt was coming home from work, and he was on his motorcycle and a drunk driver hit him dead on arrival. The driver got twenty-five years in prison, and it took Tina some time to get over it.

She also wasn't surprised that Michelle knew other things because she was a spirit a good spirit and she was going to tell Tina about the entity that Linda had seen before Tina came over. Tina needed to find a way to get rid of the demonic entities that were in the apartment.

Tina said, "Michelle the reason I'm here tonight in the apartment is because your mother, Linda called me and asked me to come over. So, when I came over, she sat down with me at the kitchen table, and she told me what she saw.

"So, I sat down across from her and she told me that she saw a little boy calling out to her she acknowledged him, and she asked him his name and he told her his name was Rodney and that he died when he was twelve in Shayne's room and that he wasn't here for her but for Nicholas. She also expressed that when she saw the back of his head she saw the bullet hole and there was green ooze dripping to her floor. He went into the room and turned around and gave an evil grin and he widened his smile, and she could see the rotting teeth in his mouth. He then slowly shut the door. She screamed.

"Then she walked slowly back to her bedroom and

slammed the door. She sat on her bed and she felt this bright light., the light was so bright it lit up her entire room and at that moment she knew it was an angel from Heaven the woman sat on her bed and they started talking about the little boy Linda saw the woman introduced herself as Maggie Marks and she continued saying that the little boy was her son and his name is Rodney and that her husband murdered her and Rodney she asked Linda to free her son from a demon that has enslaved his soul. Then they got interrupted, Maggie felt an evil presence and I was her husband and she vanished without a trace like she was never there.

"Then she was going to call me to come over and she heard loud and heavy footsteps in the kitchen it wasn't from a child she knew it was coming from a grown man so she slowly opened the bedroom door and looked and saw a man that resembled a demon from the nineties demon films but there was one big difference, he had a chunk of his head missing from the back he was bleeding everywhere she said he was smelling for another victim but he didn't see Linda, so he went into Shayne's room. Then Linda shut the door, sat on her bed, and called me to come over.

"What do you know about these entities? Why are they still here?"

Michelle knew who Tina was talking about and she gave a huge sigh. She inhaled and then exhaled.

Michelle said, "I thought those two were vanquished from floating on Earth. The father is Joshua Marks, and the woman is Maggie Marks. Maggie is unwelcome she is not to be trusted she is not an angel from Heaven she mimics the light to lure her victims she is the demon of death and whoever acknowledges her she kills them. I'm surprised the landlord didn't tell Linda and Nicholas about what happened here when the Marks were living here."

Tina couldn't believe what she was hearing. She was curious to know what happened to the Marks family and why Rodney was so evil in most cases kids who die noticeably young usually don't become evil. They are the ones that warn you that there is evil in the home and show you what you need to do but, in this case, it was different. Tina sat down next to Michelle and was eager to know what happened there.

Tina said, "Michelle tell me what happened to Rodney I need to know, and then tell me how to get rid of it. And the rest of the family."

Michelle nodded. "Okay, I will."

Tina looked at Michelle as she was starting to tell her story.

TWENTY-TWO

Michelle said, "It happened thirty years ago, the Marks family had just moved into this apartment and they had no idea what they were getting themselves into. Now Rodney knew there was something wrong with the apartment he researched the building he found out that the tenants before them were Satanists and they found a way to conjure demonic spirits spirits. It was said that the Ouija board that they used was all black and had a picture of a pentagram in the middle of the board.

One night three friends were messing with this Ouija board they made the mistake of thinking it was a game, they opened a gateway to Hell and two powerful demons came through to your world one was the High Priest of Hell, the thief of souls. His name is Valoc.

The other one is Vetis. He puts victims under his power and makes them do whatever he wants, and he does not leave until the person is dead.

Vetis corrupted their lives, and he possessed one of the friends and he made him murder the other friends, it was a murder-suicide he stabbed them to death and then he put the knife to himself. He sliced his throat and there his blood was blood was gushing out like a waterfall. He went into Rodney's room which is the same room as Shayne's he sprayed the blood that was gushing out all over the room. So, he could make demons come through the doorway from Hell on Earth.

After Rodney found out about this, he tried to warn his parents and his parents told him there's no such thing as demons, ghosts, and goblins. They told him not to talk about such nonsense, so they didn't want to hear it anymore.

On Halloween night, the household was quiet. Joshua was a police captain in the Salem Police Department. He found out two days prior that his wife was having an affair with one patrolman who happened to be his best friend. He loaded his black Beretta pistol, and he shot his wife once in the back of the head. She didn't feel anything, the bullet lodged in her head penetrating the core of her brain she died instantly. Rodney didn't hear the gunfire he was a heavy sleeper.

Joshua walked into Rodney's room and saw his son sleeping face down and a tear was coming down his right eye at direct range. He fired the weapon and the bullet went into the kid's head and lodged and penetrated the core of the brain. Rodney died instantly.

Joshua left Rodney's room, went to the kitchen table, put the barrel of the pistol in his mouth, and pulled the trigger. He died instantly."

Tina said, "Wow that's some story but why is he demonic? What happened to his spirit?"

Michelle said, "Well Maggie and Joshua were doomed before they died, they never accepted Jesus Christ as their savior. But by doing this you will not appear in the Book of Life and you will go straight to Hell. They will always be demons and serve Satan because they will never change. When it comes to Rodney, Rodney was killed in a very violent way the fact he was shot in his sleep. The Lord Jesus wanted him in Heaven but when he died someone else grabbed his soul, and he enslaved Rodney. Who am I talking about? Valoc happened. When a child dies one that is so pure and innocent like Rodney. Valoc enslaves their souls and takes control of whichever soul is easier for him to control."

"Valoc? Who is he?" asked Tina.

Michelle said, "Valoc is the president of Hell but when he appears, he appears as an innocent child and he appears to have white wings on his back and riding a two-headed dragon. He mostly appears as a child and by doing so he lures his victims his hair is short and a dark red color. He has a white face white as a ghost, and he wears a dark red suit with a white collar around his neck. Don't get fooled he is not innocent but he is extremely dangerous."

Tina was shocked about what was said to her. She was trying to take everything in and now she needed to know how to defeat them before Valoc or Rodney tried to have Nicholas.

Tina said, "How do I defeat them?"

Michelle said, "You need to take your Ouija board and

astral project yourself and free Rodney and then cast Valoc, Maggie, and Joshua back to Hell where they belong but after you do that you have to seal the room with sage and then put crosses in the room and shut the door but before you sage the room you have to get Nicholas out of there and sage him so no more spirits can come through that are evil or demonic please help my mother keep Maggie away from her. You know what to do right?"

Tina said, "Yes, I do. I know exactly what to do. Don't worry I'll take care of it."

Michelle said, "Thank you." Go back into your body and cleanse this apartment. And one more thing don't let your guard down."

Tina got up and started walking towards her body. She looked back, and she saw Michelle's spirit fading away. Then she turned back around and walked towards her body and turned around and walked backward in her body. She got her breath back.

"Holy Shit!" She spoke.

Linda said, "What?" What is it? What happened to you? I was worried."

Tina said, "We must go to Shayne's room I need to see the evil spirits. I know now what we are dealing with and what we are up against I know how we can stop it. But I need to see it first. I know the demon's name which gives us power over the entity but there are three of them. I need to see them myself."

Tina and Linda left the living room and briskly walked across the kitchen opened the bedroom door and tried to be as quiet as possible. So, both ladies got to the threshold and Tina was ready to peer through.

Tina said, "Linda perhaps you should go to the kitchen table and wait for me. If Valoc sees you he may react and that could be dangerous so I'm better off doing this part myself."

Linda agreed so she walked over to the kitchen table and sat in her usual spot, and she put her candle on the table, and she grabbed her cigarettes and a lighter and took a cigarette out of her pack, and lit it.

As Linda was patiently waiting Tina saw two entities in the room one was Joshua, and the other was Valoc he was standing behind Rodney waiting to have Nicholas. Tina saw exactly what Michelle described to her, what Tina saw next was amazing she saw Joshua walk towards Rodney he went into Rodney's soul and those two souls together were a strong combination then Valoc went into the souls, and he got bigger and stronger. He was Valoc the president of Hell all he had to do was to have Nicholas he would be the last transformation.

Tina saw a bigger and taller Valoc. He was no boy he was a huge demon that was ready to cause havoc. She saw that he had short dark, red hair, his face was white as a ghost, he was wearing a dark, red jumpsuit with a round white collar around his neck, and he had pure white wings on his back. He had a long red tail that had an arrow at the end.

Tina said, "Get away from him, son of a bitch!"

Valco was extremely angry, and his face was turning a boiling red color. His eyes started to turn red, as red as blood.

"He's mine! You can't save him or beat me. I'm too powerful for you. I have two souls in me and I'm taking

Nicholas's soul and then once I have his I will be able to stop me. Don't you know who the fuck I am? I am Valoc President of Hell. Now get out!" Valoc said.

Tina said, "I don't know who you are, and I wouldn't count my eggs before they hatch. I will beat you. I know all about you. An angel from Heaven told me who you are, and she told me how to beat you too. I intended to do just that."

Before Valoc could get the next word in, Tina got out of the room shut the door, and leftt it ajar. Then she walked over to the kitchen table, and she needed to talk to Linda about what is going on before it is too late. She sat down across the table from Linda.

Tina said, "Linda I need to talk to you about what's happening, so we can stop this demon and we need to put an end to it."

Linda said, "Okay tell me what's going on Tina don't sugarcoat it."

TWENTY-THREE

Tina put her candle on the table. "Linda, I must tell you something and it's going to sound crazy, and believe me I would think I was crazy too if I didn't see or hear it myself.

Linda had a strange feeling that she was going to say she was talking to her deceased daughter.

Linda said, "Tina did you talk with Michelle? If so, how did you do it?"

Tina leaned forward on the table. "Well let me tell you what happened to me and what the conversation was about, but before I do that I need to tell you how I was able to do so I do believe that is very important and once I tell you, I will tell you what Michelle told me after I tell you what happened I will devise a plan on how to get rid of the entity I'm going to let you know it will not be easy. What we are dealing with is an extraordinarily strong entity. He has stolen two souls already and if he possesses

Nicholas, we are in a lot of trouble he will get even stronger, and he will have Nicholas's brain. He will be smarter than any other demon I've dealt with."

Linda was staring at Tina but first, she grabbed a cigarette and lit it and she nodded. "Okay, I'm ready. Tell me the story."

Tina sighed. "The first thing I need to ask you is. Have you heard of astral projection?"

Linda said, "Isn't that an out-of-body experience?"

Tina continued. "Yes, that's exactly what it is. Your body is only a vessel without the spirit it's nothing. See I can astral project only when it is necessary to do so. Now on with the story when we went into the living room, I sensed a good spirit in the room, and I needed to find out who it was. I astral projected, so I could feel my spirit in the room, and I needed to find out who it was. I astral projected, I could feel my spirit come out of my form. I can see and talk to spirits.

"Once I was in spirit. I was looking around I saw my body and I saw you looking around right behind you I saw a shadow lingering over you he had these big red eyes he was watching us in a few minutes I will tell you about that.

"I heard this voice, an extremely sweet voice. It was the voice of a little girl. She was the most beautiful girl. She had this glow to her. She lit up the entire room. She had a personality. I knew she was in good spirits. The glow to her was so bright, calm, and so peaceful. She said hello to me, and we got talking so I asked her her name.

"She told me that I already knew her name. She told

me her name was Michelle and you were her mother. She continued to tell me that she died from SIDS.

"Then it dawned on me, and I started crying. She asked me why I was crying and she was very compassionate. So, I continued to tell her that the reason I was crying was because I could not make it to her funeral, and I explained to her that I had a job and a family. I told her that I was sorry, and she told me not to be sorry. She understood about me having that job and I had a family to support, and she knew I was a single mom, and she knew about the death of Matt. She told me that it must be hard to deal with Matt's death.

"I told her that the reason I was in the apartment was because she had called me. She saw a ghost. I also told her about the woman you saw in your room, and before that, I also made her aware of the conversation that you had with Rodney. Then I continued to tell her about when you saw Joshua in the kitchen and the green ooze and the blood on the kitchen floor. I asked her if she knew anything about these entities. I also asked about the tenants before you who were here.

"It looked like she knew exactly what I was talking about. She sighed, took a deep breath, and then exhaled.

"She told me that the family was the Marks family. She told me twenty-seven years ago, Maggie who was the wife got shot in the back of the head while she was sleeping. When Joshua was done shooting Maggie, he shot his son in his sleep in the back of the head.

"The reason Joshua shot his wife was because he found out she was having an affair with one of the police officers in the Salem Police Department. The reason he shot his son was because he would be a potential witness if he was ever prosecuted.

"Then he went to the kitchen table, put the barrel of the gun in his mouth, and pulled the trigger. Before the murders happened, Rodney knew there was something wrong with the apartment. He researched the building and the apartment he found there were tenants before them they were Satanists, and they found a way to conjure spirits," she finished.

Linda was shocked. She could not believe what Tina was saying.

"Whoa! Hold on! Are you telling me those people conjure spirits?" Linda yelled.

Tina said, "Hold on let me finish and then we can talk about how to manage this."

Linda calmed down. "Okay."

Tina continued. "It was said the Ouija board that they used was all black and in the middle of the board is a pentagram. One night three friends who lived here were messing with the Ouija board they made the mistake of thinking it was a to death and then he put the knife to his own throat, there his blood was gushing down like a waterfall, he went into Rodney's room which is Shayne's room now he sprayed his blood the one that was gushing blood from his throat all over the room and the walls.

"When he did this, blood was sleeping through the walls and it made an invisible door for the demons to come through. The room is a gateway from our world to Hell, and vice versa. After Rodney found out about this, he tried to warn his parents to tell him there were no such things as demons, ghosts, and goblins. They told him not to talk such nonsense because they did not want to hear it.

"On Halloween night, the household was quiet. Joshua was a police captain of the Salem Police Department. He found out two days prior that his wife was having an affair with one of the police officers who happened to be Joshua's best friend. He loaded his black Beretta pistol and he shot his wife in the back of the head. She did not see it coming, she did not feel anything the bullet lodged in her head penetrating the core of her brain. She died instantly.

"Joshua left the room and went to Rodney's room, and he shot him the same way he shot his wife. The bullet lodged in his brain, and he also did not see it coming. He died instantly. Joshua walked out of Rodney's room, went to the kitchen table, put the barrel of the pistol in his mouth, and pulled the trigger. He died instantly.

"So, I asked Michelle why Joshua and Rodney were so demonic, and she told me the reason why Joshua and Maggie were demonic and that is because they never accepted Jesus Christ as their Lord and Savior and she told me that anyone who doesn't accept Jesus will not go in the book of life they will not enter the kingdom of Heaven they will go directly to Hell. She also told me that Maggie is the angel of death. She appears to her victims as having a bright light and that tricks people who can see her to believe she is an angel. Anyone who acknowledges her is doomed to death. Rodney on the other hand was not supposed to be a demon. He was on his way to Heaven, but a demon grabbed his soul. When a child dies so violently and is as pure and innocent as Rodney. Valoc will enslave their soul and control whatever soul is easier for him to possess. He is a defiler. He is the thief of souls, the marquis of snakes. He is the High Priest of Hell.

"Valoc has white wings on his back, he has short red hair, his hair is as dark as blood, he wears a red jumpsuit with a white collar going around his neck and it has been told that he rides a two-headed dragon."

Linda started to cry. She was getting emotional when she heard about Rodney getting murdered the nature of the crime and the fact that the father was a captain of the Salem Police Department.

Linda said, "How do we top this son of a bitch? What do we have to do?"

Tina said, "I thought you'd never asked. Michelle told me I must use my Ouija board and astral project myself and free Rodney and then cast Valoc, Maggie, and Joshua back to Hell where they belong. After I do that, I have to seal the bedroom with sage and then put crosses in the room on the walls and shut the door but before I do that I have to get Michael out of the room and sage him so no more spirits that are evil or demonic can come through."

Linda said, "Holy Shit! What a story. That's quite a story."

Tina said, "Okay now we have to talk about what we need to do to stop these entities before they try to possess Nicholas. I need to ask you a few questions about Nicholas actually what I want is for you to tell me something about him."

Linda thought about Tina's request and she could not believe what she was asking.

Linda said, "Hey are you asking me to do this? I mean what do you need to know about him? To be honest I do not know a lot about him. I mean, he's only been staying with me for just a little over a year."

Tina said, "Well the fact that he lives with you. You know him better than I do. You see him every single day. You know his favorite food, what makes him tick and what does not, and most importantly you would know his or where he goes to church and what his spiritual beliefs are. You get my meaning?"

Linda said, "Yes, I do get your meaning. I think I can do this for you. I want to help."

Tina said, "Good I'm all ears."

Linda said, "Michael is a kind-hearted man and he would do anything for anyone. He talks about authoring a novel one day but his drinking and his excessive use of drugs always get in the middle of him doing that. Call it a roadblock. One of the things that bothers me about him is that he doesn't believe in ghosts or spirits. That sort of thing only happens in the movies and it can't happen to him."

Tina sat back in her chair and took in what Linda was telling her. She had never met anyone who did not believe in spirits, especially the ones that are demonic. She had to think about what she was going to say.

Tina leaned forward.: Linda, I want you to listen to me. I need to tell you something about what I witnessed when I went into the room. Remember when I told you it was best if I went into the room by myself? I told you to wait in the kitchen because if Valoc saw you what could happen?"

Linda said, "Yes, I do remember what you told me." There is something wrong with there? What did you see? I need to know. What's his name?"

Tina sighed out of frustration. "VALOC!"

CHAPTER

TWENTY-FOUR

"Valoc? Who's Valoc?" Linda asked.

Tina was getting aggravated because Valoc was the most dangerous demon and the hardest to defeat.

Tina said, "We have to go back to the kitchen table. I need to tell you who Valoc is what happened to him how he became a demon and how he came to our world."

Linda said, "Who cares about the history of this thing?"

Tina said, "We have to know this because we have to know how to defeat him for good but to know how to defeat him, I have to talk to someone first."

So Linda was getting discouraged, so she felt it was time for another cigarette. So, she galloped over to the kitchen table, sat at the table, took a cigarette out of her box put it in her mouth grabbed her trusty lighter, and lit her cigarette. She looked in her pack and saw she only had one cigarette left. She said, "Oh shit!"

While she was smoking Tina walked over to the living room. She went there because she could sense that Michelle was around, and the living room was where she talked about Nicholas and now she needed her help again.

Tina closed her eyes, and she could feel her spirit leaving her body and there was a bright light in the room. The light was so bright it would blind the average person and Tina could see Michelle walking towards her and sitting down on the floor Indian style she was facing the threshold. Tina walked over and sat down facing Michelle.

Michelle said, "Hey, Tina what's going on with mom? Why aren't you in the kitchen helping my mom with how to get rid of this demon?"

Tina said, "Yes I understand Michelle, but I need to tell her about this demon before we can try to stop this demon."

Michelle said, "Tell her." You know enough about this demon and where it came from and why and how he came into our world."

Tina said, "I hope she can manage this news and I will try to get prepared on how to get this thing out of her apartment."

Michelle said, "Listen this is the last thing I am going to tell you. She will be able to manage this you have done an exceptionally respectable job up to right now. Don't worry, I'll be there every step of the way. Mom won't be able to see me but deep down inside she will know I'm looking after her."

Michelle vanished and she was gone. Tina got up and

walked over to her body and her spirit went back into her body and when that happened the bright light was gone. Tina opened her eyes turned around headed over to the kitchen table and sat down.

Linda said, "So tell me what the fuck are we dealing with?"

Tina said, "Okay the name of the demon is Valoc he is the president of hell he is the right-hand demon to Satan but before that, he was a beautiful angel. He was as pure as they come but then there was Satan his name is Lucifer.

Lucifer was at the right hand of God. Lucifer was the angel of music, and he made the most beautiful music. The music he made brought other people closer to God and soothed the angels of Heaven.

So, what happened was Lucifer was trying to rule Heaven and overthrow God but that didn't work so Michael the arc angel threw Lucifer out of Heaven and into the flames of Hell. But before he did that, he grabbed angels in Heaven and forced them down with him and these angels are called fallen angels. When Lucifer grabbed those angels and dragged them to hell with him. Lucifer became Satan and Valoc became a demon and alongside Valoc was Vetis. That's the history of how they became demons. The way Valoc came through this world was through the Ouija board.

Two brothers were badasses, and they were always up to no good they went to a place called Lynn Woods and I'm sure you have heard of it. So, they thought it would be a good idea to play with this Ouija board, and when they did they had no idea what was in store for them that is how Valoc was able to get out of the Ouija board because they summoned something evil that was imprisoned in the Ouija board his name is Valoc and he killed those kids one by one and after that happened they have never seen again it was as like they fell off the face of the earth.

That was the beginning of hell on earth. Then he started to fight havoc. He was there when Chris, your son, suffocated Michelle. That's how he knew to follow you. We must stop this before it gets any worse. Before he possesses Nicholas, we must stop him. But the issue with Valoc is the only way to defeat him and cast him back to Hell is to have faith in God and if you don't it's not going to work. Then you must lock the portal and sometimes that's harder done than said."

Linda was trying to take in what Tina was telling her. She was starting to feel that she could do this, she wasn't feeling as afraid of this thing, and she wanted to finish what she started basically, she wanted to end that way so she could move on with her life.

Linda said, "Okay Tina let's get rid of this parasite that is in my house."

Tina said, "Okay let's do it."

189

TO BE CONTINUED